MEANT TO BE

LIGHT MY FIRE SERIES

J.H. CROIX

 Created with Vellum

To the detours in life.

Sign up for my newsletter for information on new releases & get a FREE copy of one of my books!

http://jhcroixauthor.com/subscribe/

Follow me!
jhcroix@jhcroix.com
https://amazon.com/author/jhcroix
https://www.bookbub.com/authors/j-h-croix
https://www.facebook.com/jhcroix
https://www.instagram.com/jhcroix/

Chapter One

PIPER

"You're breaking up with me?" I sputtered.

My seconds-old-sort-of-ex couldn't hold my eyes. He had his hands stuffed in the pockets of his jeans. When Kent finally looked back at me, I could instantly see he would be a coward about this. "If that's what you wanna call it," he muttered.

"What the hell else would it be?"

The backpack slung over my shoulder was jostled when someone walked by me at the airport. We had just landed here. We were on the way to a weekend together to watch one of my favorite bands. I'd gotten us the tickets months ago. This was one of those once-in-a-blue-moon opportunities. A popular bluegrass band was playing for the holidays at a small inn in the mountains in North Carolina.

I stared at Kent. He wiggled his jaw and shrugged. "It's been fun," he finally said.

"Fun?!" I exclaimed and threw my hands up in the air. As they fell, my backpack slid off my shoulder and landed with a thump on the floor. Someone else passing by kicked it out of the way.

I didn't even know if Kent heard me. He was already walking away. It was official. I had just been dumped in the freaking airport.

It wasn't like I thought he and I were on track to be together long-term. I had plans to move out of state soon as it was. But we *had* been dating, at least on and off for a while. We had a lot of fun together. I had tickets for a concert and a room. Just for me now.

For maybe a second, I wanted to scoop up my backpack off the floor and chase after Kent. I hated the humiliation churning in my gut. I didn't follow him. He was walking fast, quickly disappearing into the cluster of people moving through the airport like a rushing tide. We were at the airport in Charlotte, North Carolina, and I had another flight to catch. I sensed Kent already had different plans, and he hadn't bothered to tell me about them.

"I paid for your ticket, asshole!" I shouted.

If he heard me, he didn't look back. Whatever.

Someone else bumped into me from behind as they passed.

With righteous anger buzzing through me, I scooped up my backpack and fumbled for my phone in my jacket pocket. For good measure this time, I slipped both arms through the straps of my backpack, so I didn't drop it again.

"I'll just go by myself," I said to no one as I began walking.

I found a little alcove between the airport concourses with white-painted rocking chairs. Not the most comfortable seating, but I suppose they were going for the original feel. There wasn't a chair available, so I found a spot by the wall and sat on the floor.

I had three hours to kill before my next flight, which would take me to Asheville. We already had a car rental lined up. Ugh. I needed to stop thinking of "we" and realize I was on my own now. I would be driving to Merry Falls Inn for the concert all by myself.

I had just visited my older brother in

Stolen Hearts Valley, North Carolina, and gone out of my way to rendezvous with Kent here. I got the sinking feeling he had asked me to meet him here solely so I would pay for his flight. This whole holiday thing was my idea. It was supposed to be fun. I was beyond relieved I had already had my visit with my brother. He would have opinions on this fiasco.

This was just a stopping point on the way to Alaska because I was moving there. I had scouted it out during a visit with my friend Delilah a few months ago and already had my plane ticket from Asheville to Alaska after this weekend. My brother Wade would probably be gleeful if he heard Kent dumped me in the airport. He hadn't been a fan.

"Whatever, whatever," I muttered to myself.

Just then, a pair of boots appeared in my line of sight.

"Piper?" a voice prompted.

My eyes traveled upward along practical leather boots and denim-clad muscled legs to a black T-shirt and an open lightweight down jacket.

I *knew* that voice. Dylan Tayton was one of my brother's best friends. He was also inconveniently handsome and sexy.

I met his startlingly blue eyes, a contrast to his rumpled dark curls. "What are you doing here?" he asked.

"Waiting for my next flight." I stretched my legs out, crossing my ankles.

"Are you headed to Stolen Hearts Valley?"

I shook my head. "Nope."

Dylan dropped his backpack on the floor. "Mind if I wait with you?"

"Of course not."

I didn't mind Dylan waiting with me. Except I didn't want my situation to get back to my brother too quickly. He and Dylan had met when Wade was in college. They still stayed in touch. Wade and Dylan played online video games while they chatted and kept each other up to speed on everything in their lives.

"What are you doing in North Carolina?" I asked as Dylan sat down on the floor beside me.

He fished a water bottle from his backpack and took a long swallow. "Just passing through. I'm going from here to Stolen Hearts Valley, and then I'm headed up to Alaska."

My eyes whipped to his. "Seriously?"

He lowered his water bottle, setting it on

the floor. "Seriously. Why are you so surprised? I move around a lot."

I studied him for a few beats. "After this weekend, that's where I'm going."

"Seriously?" His eyes twinkled as he lobbed my question back at me.

I laughed softly as I nodded. "My friend Delilah moved out there a few years ago. I went to visit, and I loved it. Another friend who I met in vet school offered me a job at a vet clinic there. It all works out, so I'm going for it."

Dylan flashed a grin, and I tried to ignore the way my belly shimmied. "Nice. You just graduated from the veterinary program in Raleigh, right?"

"Uh-huh. Alice was ahead of me in vet school, and then I interned at a clinic where she worked. When I mentioned I was visiting Alaska, she told me about the job. So why are you moving out there?"

"I took a firefighter position on a hotshot crew. You know me, I like to travel."

"That's what Wade tells me."

I hadn't noticed my concert tickets had slipped out of the pocket of my backpack. Dylan's eyes landed on them where they lay on the floor between us. "Oh, I love the Lost Ridge Ramblers. Who are you going with?"

I wanted to play it cool. I contemplated making something up, but Wade would find out what happened one way or another, so I might as well just tell the truth. "I was supposed to go with my ex." I tried to keep my tone as nonchalant as possible, all whatever.

"Is he meeting you there?"

Dylan's sharp gaze held mine. I shrugged, feeling my cheeks heat. "He literally just dumped me here at the airport." I rolled my eyes.

Dylan's eyes widened. "Wow. What a fucking asshole."

"I agree."

He cocked his head to the side. "Is that the guy I met over the summer?"

"Dylan," I ground out. "Don't give me shit about this, and don't tell Wade."

He held his hands up. "Hey, no worries. Wade didn't really like him."

"I know he didn't." I couldn't mask the sigh that slipped out. "I never like to admit when Wade is right."

Dylan chuckled. "Fair enough. So what will you tell Wade?"

"Nothing. Not now. I'll tell him when I'm ready." I lifted my chin.

"So that's how we're gonna play this?"

"Whatever." My vocabulary was wildly

limited when I was annoyed. I let out another little huff.

He studied me. "I could go with you."

"To Alaska? You're already moving there."

"To the concert." He gestured to the tickets. "You have two tickets. I bet they weren't cheap. I hope the asshole bought them."

Yet again, I wished I could play it cool, but my grimace must've given me away.

"Aw, hell. Did you buy them for both of you?"

"We've been dating for months," I pointed out.

He let out a little whistle. After a beat, he added, "I'm sure you're embarrassed. But it's for the best, and you don't seem too heartbroken."

I rolled my eyes. "I *am* embarrassed and hurt, but I mean, it *is* for the best if he's going to pull something like that. We were just dating and having fun. I thought the concert would be fun."

Maybe it was impulsive, or maybe it was stupid and definitely foolish, but Dylan was a decent guy. Even if I sort of had a crush on him a few years ago, I was over it. We could go to the concert. I didn't really think it through when I said, "You should come with me. I have the tickets already. I have a car rented and everything."

Dylan's slow smile sent my belly into a spinning flip. He lifted a hand in the high-five position, and I slapped my palm against his.

Chapter Two

DYLAN

I stared down at Piper Ellis. With her big brown eyes, silky brown hair, and freckled cheeks, she was downright cute when she smiled. I ignored the sizzle of desire I felt whenever I saw her.

I'd had a crush on Piper ever since I'd met her. Fortunately or not, it had never gone anywhere because her brother was one of my best friends. Even though Wade and I were rarely in the same place since we'd finished college, we stayed in touch. I traveled a lot, so my path didn't cross Piper's often.

It was probably beyond reckless and foolish to propose I spend a weekend with her at this concert event. But the Lost Ridge

Ramblers were a good band, one of my favorites.

"So why are you flying through North Carolina?"

"My plan was to land in Asheville and surprise Wade with a visit."

"Does he know you're coming?" Piper asked, her eyes widening.

I shook my head. "Nope. I'll do this instead. I can swing by and see him after the weekend."

"Are you sure?" She caught her bottom lip with her teeth, sending a fiery jolt through me. I ignored it.

"I'm sure. I love this band, and I've never been able to see them live. Do you want me to reimburse you for the ticket?"

Piper laughed and shook her head. "Nope. Already paid for it. Consider it your Christmas gift from me." She paused before lifting the tickets off the floor and studying them for a moment. After she tucked them into her backpack, she asked, "When's your flight to Alaska?"

"The week after next."

She studied me before shaking her head slowly. "It's so weird we're both going to Alaska."

I ignored the sizzle of electricity I felt in

the air between us. "Definitely. Where are you headed there?"

"Willow Brook."

"Seriously?" This time, I wasn't teasing her.

She angled her head to the side. "Are you going to Willow Brook?"

When I nodded, she snorted. "It gets even weirder."

"I didn't even know you were going to Alaska," I said.

"I just accepted the job a few days ago. I'm sure you'll hear from Wade soon."

I chuckled. "I will."

"When's the last time you talked to him?"

"Last month. I just finished a stint with a crew in Montana, so we didn't have our weekly game because I wasn't online." Wade and I usually chatted when we played an online video game together. It was an easy way to stay in touch.

"Oh, that makes sense."

"So why did you fly here if you were already closer to Asheville?"

"Because I was meeting Kent," Piper ground out.

"When we get to the inn, we'll toast his goodbye," I said lightly.

She snickered. "We will. Should we get

something to eat? If you're on the same flight as I am, we have some time to pass."

"Works for me."

We stood together. I ignored the way my eyes wanted to linger on her curves as her T-shirt stretched across her breasts when she slid her arms through the straps of her backpack.

Chapter Three

PIPER

Rumor had it that plane seats were shrinking. They were small, to begin with, but I was short. This was one of the few times in the universe when being short was a benefit. Maybe the only other benefit would've been if I was skinny. I was *not* skinny. I was decidedly curvy. Most of the time, I tried to be happy with my size. But as I waited at the airport, I was feeling frumpy.

Perhaps it was getting dumped by my boyfriend at the airport when he had so clearly planned it. Or maybe it was having my brother's best friend waiting with me.

Dylan offered to drive when we conferred over the car rental situation while we had a meal at the airport.

"I'll drive. You deserve a drink," he said with a brow waggle for the ages.

"I don't need a drink to recover from Kent dumping me at the airport," I said tartly, feeling a little stung Dylan was teasing about it.

He studied me for a beat. "Are you suddenly all broken up over it?"

I felt my lips purse. My brother called it my "prissy teacher look" when I felt like this. I immediately stretched my jaw open. Dylan watched me quietly.

"No. I just said I don't need a drink to get over him."

"I wasn't implying you did," he countered pointedly. "Even if you were about to dump him, it's still shitty that he pulled this at the airport." He shrugged. "If I'd been planning a weekend with someone, even if it wasn't that serious, I wouldn't be in the greatest mood if they sketched out at the airport. Kind of cowardly, all things considered."

I rolled my eyes and snorted. "So true. Are you sure you don't mind driving once we land in Asheville?"

"Definitely not."

"I should probably add you to the car rental," I said, lifting my phone.

"Yeah, we can do that when we pick it up."

I was three margaritas in when we boarded the plane. All in all, I suppose I was grateful I had a meal before those three margaritas.

Once seated on the plane—coincidentally, or maybe not, beside each other—I glanced at Dylan. "Who knew that restaurant at the airport would have such good margaritas? I think they might be the best ones I've ever had." I smiled up at Dylan. "I feel much better," I added with a giggle and a hiccup.

He glanced down, his lips quirking with a smile. "You don't drink much, do you?"

"Nope," I said, emphasizing the P. "Do you drink a lot?" My voice was on the loud side.

A woman in front of us glanced over her shoulder as she was getting situated in her seat.

I sensed Dylan was about to laugh, but he didn't. He merely shook his head. "Not really."

When the woman glanced over again as she shimmied around whoever was in the center seat in the row in front of us, I smiled up at her, offering, "Don't worry about me. I'm very friendly."

Dylan chuckled as he slid an arm around my shoulders. "She really is."

Her gaze bounced back and forth between us, and she smiled, replying, "Y'all make a cute couple."

I was just about to blurt out that we weren't a couple when the attendant passed by, glancing down. "Can you tuck your bag under the seat a little farther?" He pointed at my backpack on the floor under my feet.

I looked up at him. "It's my footrest," I pointed out.

"Here, I'll fix it." Dylan leaned down and shifted my backpack slightly, tucking it out of the way, but I could still put my feet on it. The attendant thanked him and continued down the aisle. Dylan had removed his arm from my shoulders, but he was still *right* there beside me. With the narrow seats, I couldn't even wiggle without touching him.

Because apparently, three margaritas resulted in me saying every thought aloud, I announced, "You are *right* here." For good measure, I nudged him with my elbow playfully.

His low chuckle made my insides feel a little funny. That threw me off just enough that I didn't say it out loud. Dylan certainly didn't need to know I thought he was cute.

To be honest, he was a lot more than cute. Before I could get too caught up in this train of thought, all the stuff that happened before our plane took off set into motion. I paid close attention to the attendants as they showed us what to do if we crash-landed.

I leaned over toward Dylan, whispering loudly, "There's no ocean between here and Asheville. We're not gonna fall in the ocean."

Dylan simply smiled and reached for the pillow he had tucked in the seat pocket in front of him. He placed it on his shoulder, anticipating it was the perfect resting spot for my head.

I fell asleep. I came awake with a jolt when the wheels of the plane hit the runway. I straightened and dragged my sleeve across my cheek where I could feel some drool. I only hoped it wasn't visible to Dylan.

He glanced over. "Did you have a nice nap?"

I felt less tipsy and more normal and a little bit mortified that I had fallen asleep on his shoulder. I'd known Dylan for years and trusted him completely, but it was still weird. All of my interactions with him were always with my brother.

I wondered if I'd ever spent more than a few minutes alone with him. We had certainly spent plenty of time together. He and my brother would meet in our hometown during college breaks. He'd joined us a few other times at the lodge where my brother worked when they were hosting events there. Apparently, I still said some of my thoughts aloud before I could think better of it.

I blurted out, "We never spend time alone together. It's always with Wade."

One of Dylan's brows arched as he considered this before nodding in agreement. "You're right. Well, I guess we're getting a crash course in then. How many days together?"

I clutched the small airplane pillow to my chest. "Four days and four nights."

It was Thursday, and I had planned for us to arrive at the inn the night before the official event. The band was playing two nights there, Friday and Saturday. I had thought, very mistakenly, that Kent and I would have Sunday evening for ourselves.

Dylan was quiet for a beat before he nodded. "All right, then. Should be fun." His tone was low, and my belly shimmied. I needed to stop looking into his eyes.

Chapter Four

PIPER

By the time Dylan turned down the road that led to this inn, I was beyond relieved he was driving. It was dark, it was winter, and we were in the Blue Ridge Mountains. These mountains were famous for their winding, narrow roads. The stretch of highway that led to this inn was considered one of the world's most winding stretches of highway, known as the Tail of the Dragon. It boasted a whopping 318 curves in a mere eleven miles. They were tight, sharp, and near constant.

As Dylan rounded yet another turn, I glanced up to my side through the window. Although it was dark, I could still see the steep mountainside rising up to one side. The headlights from the rental car glittered on the icy cliff ahead. When he guided the car around another curve, the beam of headlights angled out over what I presumed was a valley. My belly felt a little funny, and it wasn't because of Dylan. I didn't want him to drive into the valley accidentally.

Apparently, I said that out loud because Dylan replied, "I'm not going to drive off the highway, Piper. You grew up around here. You shouldn't stress about this."

"I never like driving at night. Never. I did grow up around here, but it was closer to Asheville and Stolen Hearts Valley. I think I've only actually driven down this stretch of highway once. It was scary even in the daylight."

While the mountains out West in the United States were well-known for mountain passes and deep snowfall, the mountains in the East were less likely to have swathes of mountainside cut out to make way for the road. When these roads were built, they hugged the mountains and followed the curves of the landscape. Maybe we didn't get as much snow here, but the icy and wet winter was a recipe for slick roads. We had the occasional massive snowfall and ski lodges that counted on it.

Just before we turned onto the side road

leading us to the inn, we passed through a narrow stretch of the highway with steep cliffs rising on either side.

"Here's to hoping there's not a big snowstorm this weekend. I can imagine this inn gets cut off sometimes," I commented.

"Storms happen. Even if there's a big snowstorm, I'm sure we'll be fine. While we waited at the airport, I looked up the inn. They have backup generators and fireplaces aplenty," Dylan explained.

"You sound like a tourist guide," I pointed out with a snort.

I could practically feel him roll his eyes even though I couldn't see in the darkness.

"Fair enough. I like to know where I'm going and what I'm doing. I've heard of this inn before. It's famous for its year-round Christmas spirit, and it's been in the same family for generations."

In short order, we arrived at the inn. It was as cute as advertised. Merry Falls Lodge was nestled in the Blue Ridge Mountains along the winding border between North Carolina and Tennessee. It was a historic landmark, built in the 1800's.

The inn had a lovely front porch running the width of the entire building. It had a mere sixteen rooms, which was why snagging these tickets had been such a scoop. The on-site restaurant had raving reviews and promised tons of atmosphere.

Dylan's eyes arced about the space as we waited in the lobby to check in. "This is very holiday-y."

I couldn't help the giggle that slipped out. I wasn't, by nature, prone to frequent bouts of giggling. Even though they were wearing off substantially, three margaritas and the experience of getting dumped at the airport and running into my sort-of-crush brother's best friend resulted in occasional bouts of giggling.

"It's Merry Falls Inn. Christmas is totally their thing."

And, oh, was it ever. Although there were *a lot* of Christmas decorations, they were tasteful. There were wreaths and holiday lights everywhere. There was even spiked eggnog and spiced apple cider in the lobby. The entire inn was designed to get people in the spirit of the holidays.

The woman at the reception desk smiled at us. She gave off a motherly vibe.

"Well, hello! Y'all make a cute couple." Her eyes crinkled with her warm smile. "I'm Lucy Gibbins and welcome to my family's inn. If you need anything at all, just chase me down and let me know."

While I debated whether to correct Lucy on her assumption that we were a couple, Dylan chatted casually with her. She checked us in, and I was beyond relieved I hadn't listed Kent's name on this reservation. I didn't need to explain that I'd been dumped at the airport to Lucy and that Dylan was now my plus-one. I hoped that would stay my secret with Dylan, although I knew Wade would eventually find out.

Our room was on the upper floor. We passed by an archway that led into the pub where the band would perform. It was a cozy restaurant and bar with a stage at the far end. There were round tables scattered throughout the space and booths lining the walls. People relaxed while having dinner.

Although Dylan and I had wisely eaten lunch today, I was already hungry. My nerves were stretched thin between the flight, my margaritas, and the drive, not to mention the airport-dumping event. Stress tended to have opposing reactions for me. It either robbed me entirely of my appetite, or I craved food as a way to settle the jangle of my nerves.

The carpeting running the length of the hallway muted our footsteps. A moment later, we stopped at the door to our room. Maybe it was just my day, or perhaps it was just because I was beyond discombobulated with all the day had offered so far, but there was one detail I hadn't considered.

We stepped into the room. I distantly heard the thump of my backpack as it landed on the glossy hardwood floor.

"There's only one bed," I pointed out the very obvious.

DYLAN

"It's a very nice bed," I said after several beats of silence stretched between Piper and me.

I considered myself skilled at thinking ahead. With my job and life in general, I often had to plan and consider various contingencies, such as bad weather and the vagaries of wildfires. Yet this very obvious problem had not occurred to me.

I wanted to chalk it up to being tired from travel and having my thoughts otherwise occupied. Yet I knew exactly why I hadn't thought of it. Piper's mere presence had utterly distracted me. She was a living, breathing distraction. In hindsight, I didn't know what I was thinking when I told her I wanted to see this band. I *did* want to see the band—they were one of my favorites—but I knew part of it was a chance to spend one-on-one time with Piper.

She'd always been delectably cute and tempting and firmly off-limits in my mind. Wade was one of my best friends. When she was in a room, I mentally put up a wall of static. I didn't let myself think about how adorable she was.

Now, we had a single room together and only one bed.

My gaze whisked around the room quickly. No couch for me to crash on. This was a historical inn, not a hotel where they had a little suite with a sitting area and a pull-out couch. Nope. It was just us and this nice bed. It wasn't even a king-sized bed. It was a queen. There were lots of pillows and a big, fluffy white down quilt with the pillowcases a combo of red and green. The holiday spirit extended to the bedding. I was surprised holiday music wasn't softly playing in the room for us.

"There's only one bed," Piper repeated, noting the incredibly obvious.

She looked up at me, her eyes wide. "I'll go see if there's another room or maybe some kind of..." Her words trailed off as she glanced around wildly.

There was really nowhere extra to put anything. Since this was an older place, while the rooms were big enough for the bed, there wasn't much beyond that. There was just enough space on either side of the bed for the two narrow tables flanking it. A dresser sat immediately opposite the foot of the bed against the wall.

Before I could formulate a reply, she spun around and left the room. I didn't think there was another room available. According to the website, this holiday event was sold out. From my quick online perusal, this inn had events like this on the regular, drawing popular bands.

With a shrug, I eyed the bed one last time before walking into the bathroom. It was a nice bathroom with a clawfoot tub and a rainfall shower situated above it. I reminded myself Piper was my best friend's sister. I could keep my hands to myself. When I stepped back out into the main room, I eyed the hardwood floor. It wasn't inviting.

Piper reappeared, her cheeks flushed as she closed the door behind her. "There are no other rooms available. Lucy asked if we had had an argument. Can you believe that?"

I bit the insides of my cheeks to keep from laughing. "She thinks we're a couple.

Unless you want to explain, it's probably better if we just let her assume."

"Are you proposing we fake date this weekend?" Piper asked incredulously.

I rolled my eyes. "Not exactly. Lucy's friendly, but she clearly takes this whole holiday romance thing very seriously. All we have to do is not explain. That's enough."

Piper stared at me, arms akimbo as she chewed on the corner of her bottom lip. I ignored the buzz of awareness. She had a sexy mouth with a plump bottom lip and a little dip at the center of her top lip. She released her bottom lip, swiping her tongue across it.

For fuck's sake, I needed not to notice every little thing about her. The only problem was that I'd been cataloging details about Piper Ellis for too many years.

"Fine," she huffed. "We just won't fill in the blanks for anyone."

Just then, her stomach growled, and she slapped her hand over it. "I'm hungry," she announced, rather unnecessarily.

"I'm game for dinner, but I need a shower first. I've been traveling for over twenty hours."

"We can take turns in the bathroom. I don't want to wash my hair, but I could use a quick rinse in the shower."

I gestured with my hand toward the bathroom. "You go first."

Minutes later, Piper stepped out, her dark curls damp and her skin flushed. She'd changed into a fresh pair of jeans with an open blouse over a stretchy tank top. Fuck. I didn't need to notice the way her breasts stretched the fabric taut.

When I slipped past her in the narrow space between the foot of the bed and the dresser, her elbow brushed mine. A sizzle of electricity traveled up my arm from that brushing point of contact.

I started my shower cold. This weekend was going to be an exercise in restraint. I suspected this would not be my first cold shower.

Chapter Six

PIPER

I glanced around the restaurant. We had snagged the only available booth in the corner. It was tiny. Tiny enough that more than once my knees brushed against Dylan's when I moved. I shifted my feet to one side, angling slightly.

With the festive holiday decorations and the candlelight, the space was clearly designed for romance. When the server checked on us, she'd offered us complimentary champagne. I'd passed on it. I was still recovering from my three margaritas and figured I didn't need to be announcing every thought that passed through my brain again.

Dylan's hair was damp from his shower, curling at the ends along his collar. He was handsome as ever, annoyingly so. His features were a little sharper now, more defined. He had more than a five o'clock shadow. I wanted to run my fingers along his jaw and feel the prickle of his stubble. His jaw was strong and square. He had a bold nose and his brows were dark slashes. He turned to look at me, catching me studying him.

His eyes were unfairly blue. Tingles radiated from my belly, sending a ticklish feeling through my entire system.

"When did I see you last?" he asked.

Maybe he wasn't reading my mind, but it felt strange that he was contemplating the same thing.

"I think last summer."

He drummed his fingertips on the table. "That's right. I visited Wade at the lodge in Stolen Hearts Valley, and Kent stopped by."

"Mmm," I offered vaguely. I didn't want to dwell on Kent.

"His loss."

I rolled my eyes. "Thanks for coming, by the way. I'm glad you're here."

Although I definitely wasn't thrilled with the one-bed situation and felt unsettled by my reaction to Dylan, I would've felt out of place here alone. Couples were everywhere.

Dylan cocked his head to the side. "Are you really glad I'm here?"

"Yes. We're going to have to share a bed, and that's weird, but the band will be great. I wouldn't have wanted to be here alone."

Just then, our food arrived, and I was relieved. It had been a long day, to say the least.

I had ordered the pulled pork mac and cheese because I needed the carbs. A few bites in, I couldn't help but moan. "This is amazing," I said after I finished chewing.

Dylan nodded. "Seriously. No wonder this place is so popular. The food alone is worth the drive."

Dinner ended up being what I could only describe as a special form of torture. Even though I was doing my best to mentally bubble myself from paying too much attention to Dylan, it was impossible. I couldn't help but notice the way his lips kicked up at one corner before he laughed, the way his hair was a little rumpled, the way he leaned back in the booth with one forearm resting on the edge of the table, and the way his hands were strong. My gaze dwelled on his forearms. It was ridiculous. They were muscled with a dusting of dark hair. I kept noticing the motion of his throat when he swallowed. All in all, his mere existence in my vicinity with the knowledge I was about to spend an entire night in the same room with him had me twisted up inside.

I tried to remind myself that I'd just been dumped today. Honestly, I kept forgetting about that. I couldn't decide whether that was because Dylan had appeared unexpectedly in my little universe, or because it was a message from the universe that being the dump-ee was clearly what needed to happen. I should've been broken up over it. For God's sake, Kent dumped me at the airport.

In an effort to remind me of this and to scrounge up some frustration, I checked my social media channels when I went to the restroom. A suspicion that had been lingering for me, that Kent had been hung up on his ex, appeared to possibly be true. He had posted a cryptic message about visiting old friends and tagged her. Lo and behold, they were spending the weekend together. Apparently, he'd used the airline points I'd gifted him to take another flight to the coast. Great, just freaking great. I did a body check, thinking I should be heartbroken over this.

Note to self: when you wonder if you're the rebound, you probably are.

I sighed as I washed my hands in the sink. My mind immediately spun to Dylan. Maybe he was dating someone. I resolved to ask him just that.

Moments later, I was back at the booth, and he was still disconcertingly handsome and sexy. He eyed me, arching a brow, appearing to sense I wanted to ask him something.

"What's up? You look like you're pondering deep thoughts."

"You know my relationship status as a very recent dump-ee, but what's yours? Are you seeing anyone? Madly in love and engaged?"

Dylan blinked before he shook his head slowly.

"What does that mean?" I prompted.

"No, to all that," he said with a low chuckle.

I promptly decided he needed not to laugh. He had this gruff laughter that sent a shiver over my skin.

"Aren't you due?"

"Due for what?" He looked genuinely puzzled with his brow furrowing as he studied me.

"To get serious. You're a few years older than me. Wade is married," I pointed out. "You and Wade used to both be all footloose and fancy free."

"Wade never got over Dani in high school. He's exactly where he should be, happily married to the love of his life," Dylan said, his tone dry.

I couldn't help but giggle. "He *is* exactly where he should be. You're right about that. He never did get over Dani. I'm so freaking glad they both came to their senses," I said, referring to my brother and his wife. They'd been in love in high school and broken up. Wade had been so hurt, but they'd finally reconciled. "I noticed you avoided my point, though."

"I'm not Wade. There is no high school sweetheart. I'm not looking for anything serious."

"Oh, now I'm curious. Why not?"

Dylan's mouth twisted to the side as he shook his head a little. "Of course, you're curious. There's no big story; nobody broke my heart. My parents had a nasty divorce. Once you watch something that ugly, you can't unsee it. Awful is what it was. I don't ever want to go through anything like that."

"Oh." I sobered. My initial lighthearted teasing about wanting to know the backstory faded. "I'm sorry. That bad?"

He took a slow breath as he nodded. "When I was little, my parents were the kind of couple people envied, totally in love, but it blew up. My sister and I were just collateral damage."

"I've never met your sister. Where is she?"

"Alisa's actually up in Alaska. She's one of the reasons I jumped on the chance to go there. We've always been close, still are."

"Oh wow, that's really cool. I'm sorry about your parents. What happened?"

He eyed me skeptically. "This is what we're doing? Having deep conversations about our childhood?"

For the first time ever, I sensed a sharp edge with him. I wouldn't say we were close, but I knew him somewhat well by extension. He and Wade had been best friends for years. He was typically easygoing and mellow.

"You don't have to get into it. I was just curious. You know that I got dumped at the airport today, which will go down as one of my more embarrassing moments," I offered with a shrug.

He gestured toward me with a hand. "Fair enough. You know it's an old story, I suppose. My dad had an affair with my mom's best friend."

"Oooohhhhhh." I sucked my breath in through my teeth. "That bites."

"No shit. Best part?" At my nod, he added, "I'm the one who caught him."

I gasped.

"Before that, she was sort of an aunt to us, unofficially. I told my mom because I didn't know what I was seeing. It was ugly."

"How old were you?"

"I think I was nine. I didn't walk in on them having sex or anything. She was at our house when she wasn't supposed to be there and came out of the bathroom with my dad right behind her. She was in a towel. I didn't know I was supposed to be hiding anything and ended up saying something to my mom about her being there and—" He circled his hand in the air. "I don't know all the details, but it led to one hell of a fight. My mom kicked him out, and the divorce battle ensued. He and my mom's friend tried to be together for a little bit, which is why my mom fought so hard for him not to have any visits. She didn't want us to go over there. Of course, he and her friend ended up breaking up." Dylan shook his head slowly. "I still love my dad. He was a good dad, but he was a shitty husband. I think part of the reason it was so ugly was because my parents really did love each other before that. After my dad did all that and it blew up with my mom's friend, he tried to get back with my mom. It was a mess."

"I'm so sorry," I whispered.

Dylan let out a sharp breath. "Let's just say it soured me on the whole love thing."

I took in what he'd shared, my heart twisting a little. Divorce was common, but this kind of cheating was ugly. I could sense the bitterness in Dylan's voice.

"That must've been hard," I finally added, feeling like the words were wildly inadequate. For a child to be caught in the bitter transactions between parents was beyond difficult. "It must've been exhausting to feel stuck between them."

Dylan's lips twisted to the side. "That's one way to put it." He took a swallow of water. "What about you?" he asked.

"What do you mean?"

His eyes never once shifted from mine. "You know, love, romance, all that jazz? Obviously, I know your latest guy wasn't all that great, or at least he was a coward." He paused, drumming his fingertips on the table. "But then there's always knowing the whole story. Maybe you did something."

My mouth dropped open. "What?!"

He chuckled. "I'm just saying you never know. I knew a guy who got hell for walking out on his wedding. But the whole story was his almost-wife had cheated on him. They'd gone to therapy and everything. When the guy she cheated with showed up at the wedding, he walked out. Only a few people knew the whole story. He didn't care if the rest of the world thought he was a total ass. My mom wanted to tell everyone what happened, but she didn't. Even then, you can't keep that kind of affair a secret."

"I'm so sorry," I repeated.

He shrugged. "It's the past, and I can't change it. Anyway, back to you."

"I didn't do anything horrible to Kent. It's not like we were madly in love. We hadn't even talked about being in love. We were dating and having fun. I guess I just didn't expect to get dumped at the airport."

"Yeah, definitely a dick move. Should I do something to avenge you?" He grinned.

I laughed. Whether he meant to or not, Dylan's teasing about what happened started to help me let it go. Oh, for sure, it would remain a blot of embarrassment. It wasn't the end of the world. Kent and I hadn't been in love.

"It's a good story. I'd rather know now before things went further with us that he's kind of a douche."

"Guy is a total idiot. What he should've done is go to this weekend and then dump you," Dylan pointed out.

My mouth dropped open as I shook my head, laughing in annoyed wonder. "Really. Is that what you would've done?"

"Hell, no. That's even worse. I'm just saying if you're going to be a dick, then be smart about it, that's all."

I rolled my eyes. "I've never heard stories from Wade that you're a dick or a heart-breaker. Just that you're always on the move."

Dylan shrugged. "I never make promises."

Chapter Seven

DYLAN

Piper took a sip of her water, I shouldn't have noticed the way her tongue darted out to glide across her bottom lip after she set the glass down. The lighting was designed for an atmosphere, specifically a romantic atmosphere. It was soft and imbued everything with a hazy glow. With the holiday lights strung around the room and the candles on the table, the entire space was set up for love and romance.

Meanwhile, my body was strung tight with arousal, the inconvenient need tearing me up inside.

I knew the sketch of Wade's childhood with his sister. Their mother died young and their father remarried. Wade was intensely protective of Piper.

I didn't know what Piper had been through beyond that. I knew enough about life now to know that two people could experience the same thing on the outside and have it be an entirely different experience.

Piper traced her fingertips along the edge of her glass. She glanced up, her teeth catching the corner of her bottom lip and denting the plush pink surface. I took a slow breath, willing the need digging its claws into me to ease up.

"I don't know what you know about me and Wade. Our mom died in a car accident. I don't remember much about her. I like to imagine she and my dad were in love and that they had the best of it. After she died, he eventually remarried. Our stepmom was the best. Still is." Piper scrunched her nose up, her eyes shifting downward for a bit. When she looked back up, pain flickered in the depths. An unfamiliar sense of protectiveness jolted me. "I'm not that good at dating. I always end up with guys who aren't going to be there for me. Not that I'm expecting anyone to promise me forever right off the bat. I mean, that would be weird. I'm not an idiot."

"Wade says you're the smart one."

Her smile was small but warm as she looked over at me. "I think maybe I'm kind of anxious about attachment. I'm not expecting anybody to be there. Like I'm not all broken up over Kent being a dumbass because it's just how things go. I haven't sworn off love, but I don't imagine I'll ever get the fairy tale." She lifted one shoulder, letting it fall.

I suddenly wanted to prove her wrong, to make sure she understood she could have it all.

We stared at each other, and I found I couldn't look away. My heart kicked along unsteadily in my chest. The moment was snapped when the server paused by our table to see if we needed anything.

A short while later, we had finished dinner, and I was still feeling unsettled. I slipped away from our booth to go to the bathroom. I needed a moment to gather myself, to find my usual sense of distance. That wasn't something I had ever had to reach for.

You're just feeling this way because she's your best friend's little sister. That's all. Maybe it's inconvenient as all hell, but she's always been sexy and cute. You can't do anything about it, and it'll pass.

A distant voice in my thoughts almost mocked me. *It's more than that. Watch your step.*

I stepped out of the stall and crossed over to wash my hands at the sinks. A guy was already there washing his hands. He caught my eyes in the mirror.

"This seems to be the only room where you can escape the holiday spirit," he said with a dry laugh.

I chuckled. "Good point."

"I think my girlfriend expects me to ask her to marry her," he said as he turned off the faucet.

Ah, this was going to be a deep thoughts moment. "Oh?" I prompted, not sure what else to offer.

He reached for a paper towel to dry his hands. "She loves Christmas."

"Hmm," I offered vaguely.

He pressed his tongue into his cheek as he turned and rested his hips against the counter. I turned off the faucet and reached for a paper towel, thinking maybe I couldn't just leave.

"Are you okay there?" I asked as I dried my hands.

His shoulders rose with a deep breath, and he stuffed his hands into his pockets. He let out a deep sigh. "You ever been in love?"

What the fuck? It was one thing to have a

conversation with Piper about love because I knew her, but this guy was a stranger.

He seemed concerned enough, though, that I found myself answering honestly. "Nope. I'm not sure I'm the best guy for advice here. Are you in love with her?"

"I think so, but we're only twenty-two."

"Ah, well, I don't think there's an age requirement. My best advice would be, and you should take this with *many* grains of salt, if you're not ready, you're not ready. You should be able to talk to her about not being ready," I pointed out.

He sighed again.

"Another thing to ask yourself is how would you feel if you didn't ask her and that meant that was it?"

His eyes widened, almost in a panic. "I don't want that to be the end for us," he blurted out.

I chuckled. "Since I haven't been in love or ever asked anyone to marry me, I'm not the best guy for advice here. But that's the question I ask myself about big decisions, like taking a job, or moving, or anything. How would I feel if I didn't do it? Because you never do know how things will turn out. But if you're gonna wish you did, then that might be your answer. Maybe have that conversation with her."

He straightened, sliding his hand out of his pocket. "Thank you." He held his hand out to shake mine, and I reflexively took it.

"Was that good advice?" I asked after we shook hands.

He nodded. "It was clarifying. I do love her, but I'm not sure I'm ready. But if I think about not asking and that being the end of us together, well, fuck, I don't want that. I'm going to do just what you said. I'm going to tell her I'm worried, and we'll go from there."

"I'm starting to think I should charge you for that advice," I said with a slow grin.

He chuckled. "Thanks, man."

A second later, he was out the door. I stood there in the bathroom, wondering about Piper.

More importantly, I wondered how the hell I was going to get through one night with her in a hotel room, much less four nights.

Chapter Eight

DYLAN

It was late by the time we got back to the room, and I was plain exhausted. Piper stood at the foot of the bed, hands on her hips as she studied it. She spun around and opened the closet beside the dresser. "Ha! I knew they'd have extra pillows."

A moment later, she had removed the three extra pillows in the closet and lined them in the center of the bed under the covers. "There!" She looked at me with a satisfied smile. "It's like two twin beds."

I chuckled. "Sure. Whatever you say."

"Well, I didn't want one of us to sleep on the floor." She looked down at the floor in question, tapping a foot on it. "It's hard."

That wasn't the only thing that was hard.

I nodded. "It's wood. Wood tends to be like that."

When her cheeks went pink, I realized my unintentional double entendre. I flashed a grin, trying to play it off. "Just sayin'."

Hours later, I woke in the darkness. The two twin beds idea was total bullshit. Those three pillows Piper had placed between us had scattered, and I didn't know where they were. I felt one mashed up against the headboard between us. Between our bodies was nothing. Piper slept in a large loose T-shirt and a pair of leggings. She was plastered to my side with one of her legs draped over mine. I could feel the plush give of her breast against my rib cage.

I lay still, trying to will my body to calm the fuck down. Piper shifted beside me, making this sweet little sound in her throat and letting out a sigh. She cuddled a little closer to me.

I gritted my teeth, my eyes wide open in the darkness as I stared up at the ceiling. I started counting imaginary sheep. I eventually gave up and carefully slid away from her, moving in increments, relieved when she remained asleep. I felt the mattress shift as I rolled carefully to my side. I brought my feet to the hardwood floor. It was cold and decidedly hard. I knew I wouldn't have had a good night's sleep there, but it was clear I probably should've opted for that.

Once I stood, I waited, listening to the sound of Piper's breathing. It never shifted out of its slow, steady rhythm. I took a quiet breath in the darkness before padding with stealthy footsteps into the bathroom and closing the door behind me. My cock was so hard I didn't even think I was going to be able to go to the bathroom. I turned on the shower, stepping into the icy cold blast of water.

Even though it probably made the most sense to take matters into my own hands, literally, I couldn't bring myself to do that. Not with Piper through that thin wall in the bed on the other side.

For fuck's sake, she was my best friend's little sister.

The cold shower did the trick. By the time I stepped out, I was wide awake, but things had shriveled up, so to speak. I chuckled to myself. That should keep me sane through to the morning.

Chapter Nine

PIPER

"Oh, come on. Let's go together."

Dylan had suggested we go skiing today. Fresh snow had fallen the night before. Although the inn wasn't a ski lodge, he, of course, knew of some backcountry trails nearby.

"Where are we going to get our skis?" I asked what I thought was the obvious question.

"I already checked with Lucy. She told me where we can rent some just down the road. Let's go for it. Just for a couple of hours. It'll be fun. Unless you want to stay here by yourself in the room."

I didn't want Dylan to know my pointless secret. I might've grown up in the mountains here, but I'd never been great at skiing. Not like my brother. I'd had a bad skiing fall once in high school and had been a little nervous about it ever since.

I decided to tell him the truth and braced myself for some teasing. "I had a scary fall while downhill skiing in high school. I'm not good at it."

"We'll just stick to the cross-country ski trails. Nothing downhill. I promise."

"But..."

He rested his hands on his hips as he studied me. "I promise. Just level trails. Maybe it'll be a good experience."

I blinked. "Okay, fine."

As we were walking out a few minutes later, I glanced over. "I thought you would tease me."

Dylan glanced down. "Not about that. I've done a lot of guiding over the years. Everybody has their fears, and it's not cool to tease. If you really don't want to go, we don't have to." He stopped by the rental car.

"Let's do it!"

His grin sent my belly into a dizzying swoop, and off we went.

A short while later, cross-country skis and gear rented, Dylan stood beside me. He leaned down to check that I was secured to my skis. "You're good."

He kept his promise. We stayed on flat, easy trails with nothing more than gentle slopes here and there. We stayed out for more than two hours. By the time we were done, I felt bracingly alive in the crisp winter day and not the least bit anxious.

When we skied to a stop at the trailhead by the parking area, I glanced over with a smile. "Thank you."

Dylan looked over at me, lifting a hand to remove his hat. "For what?"

"This." I swung my arm toward the trail behind us. "It isn't that I haven't skied at all since that fall, but not very much. This was fun."

"Anytime. I prefer cross-country skiing to downhill. Once we're in Alaska, I'll go with you if you ever want to go. We can stick to the flat trails or find something a little more challenging."

My belly swooped as his gaze held mine, and my pulse started to buzz faster. I kept trying to tell myself this super-inconvenient attraction to him would fade. But it wasn't. Not at all.

I could hardly even bear to think about

how I'd felt waking up during the night deeply aroused, beyond hot, and bothered. I'd been plastered to his side. I'd been so relieved it was close to morning that I practically leaped out of bed and raced into the bathroom.

"Let's get back to the inn." Dylan removed his gloves and checked his watch. "We've got time for an early dinner before the first concert tonight."

I told myself the rush of seeing one of my favorite bands live in a small setting like this would distract me from Dylan. Between skiing today and the concert tonight, I would be exhausted.

Chapter Ten

PIPER

The band's performance was even better than I could've imagined. Guests crowded the pub. Dylan and I were off to the side, dancing with most of the small crowd.

Maybe it was getting into the spirit of it—between the holiday, the band, the pure adrenaline of it, along with being surrounded by couples—but somewhere along the way, I looked over at Dylan. Our gazes linked and it felt as if electricity zapped through the air between us, sizzling straight through me.

I instantly burned up inside. Seconds later, someone bumped into me, shoving me into Dylan. He steadied me with an arm around my waist. The next thing I knew, we were dancing together. The band shifted from a rollicking tempo to a slow, bluesy song at that moment.

I had stripped out of my blouse and left it on the back of my chair. I was down to a silky tank top because it was hot and crowded. When I met his eyes again, seriously caught up in the moment, I impulsively leaned up to kiss him.

We were laughing as our lips met. My brain cells went poof. His lips molded to mine as I let out something like a whimper and arched up against him. His palm slid down to curve over my bottom, pulling me flush against his body. I was suddenly aware of his arousal. OMG.

Our kiss went on and on and on as we swayed together. We finally broke apart, staring at each other with wide, stunned eyes.

"Oh my God," I rasped.

I felt the gust of his breath. "That's one way to put it."

I scrambled for composure, for any semblance of sanity. Before I could pull myself together, his palm stroked my spine, and his fingers laced into my hair. "Piper," he growled just before his mouth claimed mine again.

This time, his kiss was purposeful, masterful. I was burning up, nearly shaking with need. This kiss was like gasoline poured on an already raging fire. The flames burst skyward inside.

We were beside the wall and stumbled against it. Without it, I probably would've fallen to the floor, weak-kneed in a puddle of pure desire.

His hand slid through my hair and down to cup one of my breasts. He rocked his hips into mine, and I let out a needy whimper, my hips rolling to meet his.

I had no idea how long our kiss lasted by the time we finally broke apart again. We stared at each other, breathing raggedly.

"Fuck, Piper," Dylan murmured.

I felt cheeky and so wildly out of control that I didn't think when I replied, "You could do that."

He let out a sharp bark of a laugh.

Chapter Eleven

DYLAN

After we returned to our room, Piper and I studied each other across the bed.

"Uh, that was crazy," she offered.

I nodded slowly. I was still aroused, my cock swollen and pressing against my zipper.

"What if—" She began but then abruptly turned away. Long seconds ticked by before she turned back. "It would be crazy, right?"

We had already crossed the threshold of crazy, but I knew what she meant. We could chalk up that crazy kiss to being caught up in the moment. If it went further, we might have a problem.

I shrugged. Because at this point, I wasn't thinking clearly. At all. All I knew was I wanted Piper. I wanted to see this through. I wanted more.

"Let's just go to sleep," I finally said, clinging to some kind of sanity, a thread of propriety.

Piper was Wade's little sister. I couldn't fuck her. Even though she had specifically said I could.

We went to bed. Once again, despite that silly wall of pillows, I woke in the night with Piper plastered to me. This time, my arm was wrapped around her waist, and my palm was covering the sweet little curve of her bottom.

I'd never let myself think about Piper much. In fact, I trained myself around her not to notice much. She was cute as hell and just the kind of woman I craved—with generous curves and more cute than pretty.

She shifted against me, and I felt when she came awake.

Fuck it. You've already messed this up. Might as well make the best of it.

I could try to play it cool. But we had already kissed. We already agreed that was crazy.

If she moved her knee even an inch, she would brush against the tire rod of my arousal.

"Dylan?" she whispered in the darkness.

To let her know I was awake, I squeezed her bottom. Her breath hissed. "Dylan!"

"What? We already kissed. Plus, this is the second night I've woken up like this with you."

I felt the curve of her smile against my shoulder where her head was tucked. She shifted, moving that knee. Whether she did it on purpose or not, I didn't know, but I heard her startled breath.

"Can't hide it," I said into the darkness.

"What do you mean?"

"Piper, I want you. I want to fuck you," I said bluntly. "Even though it's a really bad idea."

"It *is* a bad idea, isn't it?" She moved again, and I felt her palm land on my chest. She rested her chin atop it.

My heart rampaged in my chest, and I ached with need. For my best friend's little sister. *Fuuuuuuuck.*

All of that would've been bad enough, but now, it was dark and we were in bed together. Instead of being sensible and rolling away from me, even maybe rebuilding the stupid pillow barrier, Piper remained where she was. I could feel every inch of her where she pressed against my side. I could feel her expectant gaze on me.

No doubt she could feel the reckless pounding of my heart underneath her hand. I could feel her own heartbeat where she pressed against my side.

I'd gone to sleep in a T-shirt for the second night in a row. I didn't usually sleep in a T-shirt, but I also didn't usually end up in a bed with Piper, a woman I wasn't supposed to want. Yet my body ignored logic and reason. Rules didn't apply in the suspended moment where we resided.

"What if...?"

I had to bite the inside of my cheeks to ask what she meant.

The bathroom had a night-light beside the sink that remained on. The little glow of light reflected off the mirror immediately across from the bathroom, offering just enough light in the bedroom for me to see her face.

"What if what?" I finally asked when she snagged her bottom lip with her teeth, worrying it just enough to send a hot sizzle of need through me, like lightning streaking across the sky before a summer storm.

I felt her shrug when she lifted one shoulder.

"We already kissed," she pointed out.

I had to force myself to breathe a little more slowly. "We did."

"It's just one weekend."

I felt a little chuckle rumble up in my throat. "It is," I agreed.

My heart kept on knocking against my ribs, hard enough to crack one. All the while, my cock throbbed. I could literally feel my pulse down there.

"You don't want anything more. I don't either."

Fuck me.

"Your brother would kill me," I felt pressed to point out.

Piper's eyes narrowed. "Wade has no say over any of this."

I couldn't help but grin at how offended she looked.

"I'm not saying that Wade has any say over who you're involved with, or me, for that matter. I'm just saying he's one of my closest friends. He would be pissed at me."

Her breath drew in sharply. "Fuck Wade. I don't care what he thinks. That's it." Her fist curled to press firmly on my chest.

For a split second, I thought she'd been struck with a dose of sanity.

But no, I was wrong. So very wrong.

She shifted up, announcing, "I'm kissing you again."

Before I could even form a thought, I felt her lips, soft and lush, her tongue instantly slipping in to tangle with mine.

Oh, fuck me. It wasn't that I wanted to resist. Hell fucking no. I wanted Piper. I wanted this. I wanted all of her.

I let out a rough groan into our kiss. She shimmied closer and straddled me. Her hips centered over the rock-hard ridge of my arousal. She gave a little wiggle in emphasis, and I gripped her hips with my hands, rocking up into her.

She gasped into our kiss and then broke away. We stared at each other in the dim reflection of light from the bathroom.

There was absolutely no doubting the depths of my raw and fierce lust for Piper. But at this moment, something else shimmered between us, something startling—a sense of intimacy, of connection, of closeness.

Her eyes searched mine. I tried to grasp onto some discipline. But all thought, all reason, all logic had gone up in smoke the second she straddled me. She moved her hips again and I could feel the heat of her arousal through the thin cotton of my boxers.

"Piper," I bit out when she rocked again.

My hands tightened on her hips. Everything about her felt so fucking good, so fucking perfect, so fucking tempting. Her hips were soft and lusciously curved. I savored the give of her softness when I squeezed.

"What?" she rasped.

"I don't know if this is such a good idea," I managed to say on the heels of a ragged breath as I scrambled for some semblance of control.

"Oh, it's a bad idea. But I don't care. We've already crossed into awkward. Let's make it worth the trouble."

Chapter Twelve

PIPER

I almost didn't recognize this version of myself. I'd thrown all caution into the wind and locked the door behind it. I was reveling at this moment. I felt wild, unbridled, and downright wanton.

My pride was possibly, just a little stung by getting dumped at the airport. I hadn't seen Kent in over a month because he'd been out of town for work. We were supposed to just have a fun weekend.

In the aftermath of his cowardice, it was as if the universe had decided to give me a little gift to make up for it. Dylan landed in my world. Literally. Now, here we were.

He was just as sexy and delectable as he'd

always been. Wade had no fucking say in my life. Not who I kissed, not who I wanted, and most definitely not who I had a fling with. Dylan and I had three more nights together. We might as well make the best of them.

I ran my palms over his muscled chest and down over his abs to the hem of his T-shirt. Dipping under it, I found his skin warm. I slid my palms up, savoring his muscled planes.

Dylan's eyes held mine. "Are you sure about this?"

Even his voice got to me. It was always low and a little rough, with just a hint of a Southern twang.

I rocked my hips a bit, feeling a sharp jolt of pleasure. "I'm absolutely sure."

"Piper—" My name ended with a groan when I shimmied over his cock again.

I was teasing us both, and I gloried in it. "What?" I asked.

His hands gripped my hips tightly, holding me still when I went to move again.

"Of course, I want you. Hell, I've wanted you for years." My eyes widened at that. He chuckled. "You're fucking hot and sexy and cute. I've always thought it was convenient I didn't see you that much. The temptation might've been too much. But—" He closed his eyes, letting out another ragged breath before opening them again.

"But what? We've known each other for years. I trust you, and I want you. I don't want to be sensible."

"You just broke up with your boyfriend."

I rolled my eyes. "He dumped me. At the airport. And it wasn't like we were serious. We didn't even live in the same place." My hands were still on Dylan's chest under his T-shirt, which had ridden up to the bottom of his rib cage. "It wasn't serious, and we weren't in love. I'm moving to Alaska, so that would've put an end to it as it was. Don't get all in a twist about it. I hadn't seen him in over a month."

I leaned down, pressing a kiss on the side of his jaw before moving close to his ear, whispering, "Fuck me, Dylan."

That seemed to do the trick because he gripped my hips tightly and rocked up into me. I shivered all over at the sweet pressure on my clit.

We tumbled into another kiss, and I forgot everything but Dylan. Our kisses went on and on and on. Somewhere along the way, his hands slipped under my shirt. He groaned into my mouth as he broke away, his palms sliding up to cup my breasts. His thumbs teased over my nipples.

"Fuck, I've wanted to feel your skin for too damn long, Piper," he murmured.

I straightened, catching the hem of my T-shirt and lifting it over my head in a big swoop, then tossed it to the floor behind me. My breasts bounced slightly with the motion.

He leaned forward, catching one of my nipples with his mouth. I cried out at the warm, wet suction. Sharp, piercing sensation arrowed to the core of me.

"We need to get naked," I announced.

I didn't want to get off him, but there was only one way to do this. I rolled to the side as I shimmied out of my pajama bottoms. They were thin flannel cotton with penguins all over them.

Dylan sat up and threw his T-shirt to the side. He rolled off the bed, tossing over his shoulder, "Be right back."

I was about to ask where I was going, but a few seconds later, he reappeared, throwing a condom onto the small table beside the bed. He kicked off his boxers, and I swallowed at the bare-naked sight of him.

He was a hotshot firefighter. The job demanded he be in shape. Even though I was prepared, the view sucked my breath right out of my lungs. Every inch of him was muscled and fit, and his cock was thick.

I was just sitting there on the bed. I couldn't think for too long. On the heels of another fiery second, I felt the mattress dip. Dylan stretched out beside me, sliding his palm over my belly.

The look in his eyes encompassed all of me. "Piper," he rasped as he bent to catch my mouth in a kiss.

I could've kissed Dylan for days upon days. He was thorough and dallied, teasing me with his tongue. Drawing away to nip my bottom lip and dropping kisses on the corners of my lips, he practically made love to my mouth.

He made love to all of me, dusting hot kisses on my neck, along my collarbone, and down between my breasts before catching one nipple and then the other with his mouth, his teeth grazing just enough to make me moan.

I was a bundle of need and gasping and crying out. Each kiss on my trembling belly felt like hot drops of sweet syrup on my skin. I felt his palm sliding up my thigh, pressing my knee out to the side. His fingers teased into the core of me. He murmured a sound of satisfaction.

"Oh, sweetheart, you're so wet."

All I could do was gasp when he sank two fingers into me just before bringing his mouth to my sex. Dylan proceeded to drive me absolutely out of my mind. He made love to me, fucking me slowly with his fingers, teasing pumps in and out as his tongue explored my folds.

Just when I thought I would lose my mind, he said, "Come for me, sweetheart."

I could feel his words on my pussy just before he sucked lightly on my clit. My orgasm shattered me. I cried out, calling his name between ragged breaths.

I hadn't even recovered, pleasure still rolling through me in swirls and eddies as he drew away. I managed to drag my eyes open, watching as he rolled the condom on.

At another moment, he caught my hands in one of his and stretched them over my head. My breasts jutted up as his weight came over me. He reached between us, notching his thick crown at my entrance.

I was slippery wet with my arousal coating my thighs. He held my gaze, asking, "Are you sure?"

"Yes!"

I watched as he took a breath and slowly filled me. My heart thudded, and I couldn't look away. I was caught up in an intense rush of need and desire, all of it tangling within a startling intimacy.

Chapter Thirteen

DYLAN

My heart pounded so hard in my chest that I could hardly breathe. One beat rolled into the next, a crescendo that swept me in its wake.

Piper's gaze was locked with mine. Her skin was soft and dewy. Sheathed in her slick, rippling core, I was caught in a fast-moving current of sensation. Desire and fierce need bound within a shocking sense of intimacy.

I held still for several beats of my heart. She made this little sound as her hips rocked up toward mine.

The momentum took over, and we hurtled forward. I thrust into her again and again as she rose to meet me every time. Until then, I had been clinging to some control, maybe just barely. Once the rush took over, there was no finesse. It was all a mad dash.

I felt her begin to quicken underneath me. Releasing one of her hands, I fumbled to reach between us, teasing my fingers over her clit. She cried out. All finesse aside, I'd lucked into giving her just enough pressure that she came again. Her entire body trembled, quivering underneath mine as her channel tightened around me.

"Dylan!" she gasped.

That toppled me over the edge. The release, sizzling like lightning waiting to strike, snapped through me with such force that all I could do was cry out. We shuddered together, and I fell against her. For a moment, I was stunned, collapsing without even an ounce of energy to keep my weight off her.

After a few deep breaths, I collected myself. I had enough wherewithal to scramble together enough energy to move, shifting to my side and curling an arm around her back to bring her with me.

I couldn't even speak. I'd had great sex before. It wasn't that which left me speechless. It was the raw, emotional intimacy I felt with her. I almost couldn't face it. It felt as if

I'd been cleaved wide open. Even more startling, I knew Piper experienced it too.

We'd been caught in it together, a net cast around us, shimmering with sparks and light and an undeniable connection.

Piper moved first, eventually lifting her head. We studied each other in the shadowy light.

"Oh," she finally said.

One of my hands rested between her shoulder blades. I could feel her heart beating with the pace of it gradually slowing, in tandem with my own.

"Oh," I echoed back to her.

Maybe it should've been incredibly uncomfortable, but it wasn't. I felt too stripped bare to talk much. We disentangled ourselves, and I slipped out of bed to dispose of my condom in the bathroom.

Piper took her turn in there after I came out. We crawled back into bed together. She didn't make the pillow barrier, and I couldn't help but tease.

"No pillow wall?" I asked as the bed dipped under me when she slipped under the covers.

She rolled to face me, and I saw the curve of her smile against her cheek. "It seems kind of silly now."

"Oh, it was silly before."

She cuffed me lightly on the shoulder. Without thinking about it, I coaxed her closer as I curled an arm around her back. She didn't resist, softening against me.

Her plush curves pressed into my side. I wasn't much of a cuddler. In fact, the last woman I'd dated had complained about it. She'd said I wasn't affectionate enough, and she felt like I just wanted sex.

I'd never experienced the urge to be affectionate like this. Here, in the darkness with Piper, I didn't want to question it. My cynical mind waited in the quiet shadows, looming there to remind me of all the reasons it was stupid to let myself fall for anyone.

Chapter Fourteen

PIPER

The following day, there was chatter about a storm rolling in. It was supposed to bring the dreaded wintry mix of snow and ice.

I brushed away any worries. We were here for this weekend with good food, good music, and good company. I wasn't even letting myself think about the fact that Dylan and I had showered together this morning or what he had done to me with his fingers while we were in there. The man was talented.

Maybe it was the two orgasms. Orgasms tended to put me in a good mood. We didn't need to think about me kneeling at his feet in the shower, the water from the shower rolling down my back as I brought him into my mouth and teased him to a climax.

He seemed to be in a good mood too. We went down for the buffet-style breakfast, met some of the other guests, and chatted. Dylan and I considered going cross-country skiing again but decided against it because of the weather. We both knew icy roads in the Appalachian Mountains could be dangerously treacherous. The threat of black ice was always there. With rain mingling with snow on the winding mountain roads, those conditions could spell disaster.

Perhaps it was because I had known Dylan for years, but I trusted him. He was my brother's best friend. No matter what happened, he wouldn't be an asshole. Neither of us had expectations. Not even a little.

Here and there, the reality that we were both moving to Alaska feathered along the edges of my thoughts, reminding me of the possible complications. But I didn't need to think about those.

"Are you ready?" Dylan's voice broke into my train of thought.

I glanced over. He stood in the doorway to the bathroom in our room. We planned to head back downstairs.

I set down my hairbrush as I smiled over at him. "Whenever you are."

His eyes held mine, the look there warm.

My belly shimmied, and my pulse started to speed along. He glanced down. "You need some shoes."

I rolled my eyes as I walked past him, bumping my shoulder against his. "They're here." I stepped into them.

When I turned, he was *right* there. He took a step closer, and my back bumped against the wall.

My insides went molten at the heat flashing in his eyes. I barely sucked in a breath when he took one more step. I felt the heat of him like a blast from head to toe. "What are you doing?" I asked breathlessly.

"This," he said before he bent low and brought his mouth to mine.

He cupped my cheeks as he bent low. It was just a kiss. Our tongues twined together just once before he lifted his head. His hands remained on my cheeks as he stared into my eyes.

I whimpered. The moment passed quickly, but I felt as if a link held between us, catching on my heart and cinching tight. I was almost off-balance when he stepped back and reached for my hand.

I didn't know what we were doing, but we were together for this unexpected weekend. I savored the feel of his hand around mine as we walked down to where we could hear the band warming up.

The band was mid-set when everything went black. The sound of the wind howling outside whipped through the suddenly quiet space. Someone in the band called out, "Power's out!"

After another shuddering gust of wind, Lucy called out from the bar, "We have backup generators that power the heat and lights. We'll need to keep the heat lower than usual so we don't overwork the generators. Power's out to the whole area."

Everyone shifted into motion, milling about before people began organizing things. Fires were lit in the massive fireplaces in the public rooms. Each room had backup heat and some lighting, but the pub area was the warmest room.

Dylan and I went to bed with the heat on low. I awoke during the night, snuggled tight against his side. I sensed he was already awake.

"Dylan?" I whispered in the darkness.

"Yeah?"

"I'm glad you're here."

He was warm, like my own personal furnace. Even though Lucy assured us that the generator would run the heat for up to a week with the amount of fuel they had stored, that meant keeping the temperature lower. It was chillier than I was accustomed to.

"I'm glad you're here too," he replied in a rumbly voice.

He slid his hand in a slow pass down my spine, curving over my bottom. I was already aroused. That was apparently my state when I was in bed with Dylan. My body simmered on low burn all the time.

"How long do you think it'll be before they get the roads cleared?"

"A few days," he replied, sounding unbothered. "There's more than one area to clear."

I instinctively snuggled closer to him, and he gave my bottom a little squeeze.

I wanted more. I turned my head where it rested in the curve of his shoulder, pressing a kiss just above his collarbone. We explored each other in the darkness, hands and lips teasing and touching. Every touch felt intensely intimate in the darkness.

When he shifted to roll me on top of him and said, "Ride me, sweetheart," I did just as he asked, crying out when I felt the thick, delicious slide of him filling me.

His fingers pressed into my hips. He

shifted back into the pillows against the headboard, levering me closer and creating the perfect angle of friction where we joined. Each subtle thrust sent piercing pleasure through me.

On the heels of a deep surge, I cried out, crying his name in a ragged gasp as pleasure ricocheted through me.

I felt him shudder against me, savoring the sound of my name as he came in a gruff shout. When I relaxed against him, he sifted his fingers through my hair. I soaked in the light touches after it was over.

He tucked the covers over us together after he went to the bathroom. I was drowsy and sated and fell asleep thinking I could stay there forever.

Chapter Fifteen

DYLAN

I woke up with Piper cuddled up to my side. Again. We'd gotten the extra blanket out of the closet. I could hear the hum of the generators. Meanwhile, the wind still rushed through the darkness. The icy snow and rain pinged sharply against the windows.

Piper felt good. This—with her—felt shockingly good. My thoughts scattered. I wanted to chalk up the way I felt to really great sex. Sex with Piper was better than great.

But *this*, waking in the night with her curled warm against my side, layered something else into it. It felt as if these encounters were a tide rolling in on a sandy beach. The grooves of cynicism in my mind and heart were washing away wave after wave.

Piper shifted against me, making this sweet little sound in her throat, a soft, satisfied sigh before she snuggled even closer to me. My arm wrapped around her back, with my palm resting on the curve of her hip. I reflexively stroked in a lazy circle, savoring the feel of her silky skin. I wanted to protect her but from what I didn't even know. Maybe it was the storm, or perhaps it was the rocks life kicked in our path. At this moment in the darkness, nothing mattered other than keeping her warm and safe with me. I fell back asleep.

Light filtered through the windows when I woke again, and I rolled my head to the side to look out. The wind was finally slowing, and the sky had begun to clear. I could see slivers of light breaking through the thick cloud cover.

"Is the storm over?" Piper's voice was soft, the edges frayed.

I glanced down to feel her lifting her head from my shoulder. Her hair was tousled and messy, and my heart felt pierced with a sharp sweetness.

Without thinking, I lifted a hand,

brushing her hair away from her cheek. "Looks like it's almost over," I offered.

She blinked, her eyes shifting from me to looking out the window. "I wonder how long it will take them to clear the road."

I shrugged, thinking I didn't even care. I just wanted to be here in this cocoon, sheltered away from the world with Piper.

When we rolled out of bed a few minutes later, it was chilly in the room. The staff had notified us last night that the water would be cold if we wanted to shower.

"What do you think about showering?" I asked.

Piper rested her hands on her hips, eyeing the shower. "Let's make it really quick. I can only handle so much cold water. I just need something to freshen up."

A few minutes later, we raced through the gauntlet of a bracingly cold shower.

"I'm awake." She grinned as she looked over at me.

We got dressed and headed down to the main area. We discovered some guests had piled blankets in one of the main rooms. A fire crackled in the large fireplace, and the kitchen was in full swing. Staff were setting up the buffet, and a radio played.

"Any news?" I asked one of the staff members.

"They're saying at least two more days. We're going to make it entertaining. The rooms might get a little colder, but people can bunk down here if they want. We have tons of food."

The atmosphere felt fun. Everybody hunkered in to make the best of getting stranded by the winter storm. They rearranged the tables to leave space in front of the large fireplace. We found a table by the windows. While the wind was still whipping, the clouds broke apart to show more blue sky.

Another couple glanced around, looking for a table. I looked over at Piper. "We should let them sit with us."

"Of course!" She waved them over.

"Plenty of room here," I offered when they stopped by the table.

They sat down, smiling at us. "I'm Matt," one guy said, with the other chiming in, "And I'm Jack."

"I'm Dylan," I replied, just as Piper responded, "Piper. Nice to meet you both."

"How did y'all sleep last night?" Matt asked.

"Pretty good," Piper said. "We got the extra blanket out of the closet."

"Same here," Jack said. "It seems like some people opted to come down here."

"It's like camp," Matt quipped. "Do you think the band's going to play tonight?"

"I heard they're going to do an acoustic show," I said, having gotten that tidbit from Lucy.

"They're scheduled to play tonight anyway," Jack commented. "After tonight, that's just a bonus show if we're still stranded. I hope the food holds out."

"Lucy said there's enough food for over a week," Piper added.

"We could organize charades and other games," Matt said.

Piper grinned. "I love that!"

"Are y'all from around here?" Jack asked.

"I grew up in Stolen Hearts Valley, but I don't live there anymore," Piper replied.

"I'm from Colorado, but I've lived all over the place."

"What brings y'all here?" Matt prompted.

"The band is one of my favorites," Piper explained. "Dylan and I thought it would be a fun weekend. What about y'all?"

"We're from Asheville and also here for the band. I would guess pretty much everybody here this weekend is here for the band," Jack replied.

"Where do you live now if you're not in Stolen Hearts Valley anymore?" Matt asked.

"We're both moving to Alaska," Piper replied, glancing at me.

Jack's brows hitched up. "Well, Alaska is definitely a change of pace from here."

"Bigger mountains and longer winters." I chuckled.

We chatted with them, learning they ran a furniture business in Asheville. We even exchanged numbers, assuring them we would send pictures from Alaska once we were there.

The wind buffeted the inn all day, and icy rain fell periodically. We ended up having an enjoyable day. The guests set up a schedule for bringing in wood for the fire. Matt and Jack also organized games and a no-money-allowed poker tournament.

When evening came around, the band played an acoustic show. As we rolled into the third day there, I looked over at Piper. My heart felt as if someone had knocked it off its feet. I'd stumbled and lost my balance emotionally. Perhaps it was how unexpected the situation was. I wasn't even supposed to be here.

Maybe this thing with Piper had sent me spinning inside. That evening, we sat in a circle on the floor near the fire. This was definitely the warmest place in the inn by this point. The rooms hovered around fifty degrees. I'd opted out of this card game while she played slapjack with Jack. They were laughing hysterically.

Eventually, Piper won and thrust a fist in the air. When she caught my eyes, her cheeks were pink, and her eyes were bright. I wanted to lean over and kiss her. Considering we were continuing the ruse of truly being a couple, I did.

Her smile was warm when I lifted my head. For just a moment, my heart gave a shuddering kick. We stared at each other while I was caught in the dawning realization that we weren't faking it. Her hair was up in a messy ponytail. I wanted to loosen it and slide my fingers through her silky locks while I kissed her senseless.

I straightened, looking away at the fire. When I glanced around, my eyes landed on Jack while he shuffled the cards. He smiled at me, offering, "Y'all sure make a good couple. How long have you been together?"

Piper and I looked at each other. Matt and Jack were our friends at this point. Piper shrugged. I decided to let her answer, unsure what she might say.

"Just the weekend. We've known each other for years because Dylan's one of my brother's best friends. They went to college together, and they're both firefighters," she explained.

Jack looked back and forth between us. "Just the weekend?"

Piper's gaze slid to mine for a beat before she rolled her eyes. "I kind of got burned. But I already had the tickets for the weekend, and Dylan offered to join me. To be honest, I've always had a crush on him, so we decided to just have this weekend."

When Matt and Jack glanced my way, I nodded. "That's the deal."

Jack's lips kicked up at the corners. "My point stands. Y'all make a good couple, and you're both moving to Alaska. Maybe you should make it more than just this weekend."

Matt, who appeared to be the quieter of the two, flashed us a smile. "Jack is a matchmaker."

"For real?" Piper asked. Jack passed her the deck of cards, and she began shuffling them again.

"I run a matchmaking service as a secondary job. It's not the usual thing," he explained.

"What is it, then?" Piper pressed.

Jack looked pensive as he glanced at Matt, who nudged him with his knee. "Just tell them."

"My father was a pastor, and he did marital counseling for couples before marriage." Jack rolled his eyes. "It was kind of funny because he wasn't supposed to tell people if he didn't think they would work out, but he did. He was usually right. To clarify, I'm not a pastor."

"Definitely not," Matt chimed in as he waggled his brows.

Jack chuckled. "I'm also not a counselor. I started a thing where couples can sign up to chat with me. I do their astrology chart, we do a whole thing, and I give them feedback on who I think may be a good fit for them. I don't know much about y'all, but you'll make it." He paused, his gaze sobering. "But before you can do that, you have to believe it."

Chapter Sixteen

PIPER

You have to believe it.

Jack's pointed observation kept bouncing back into my thoughts. This weekend was turning out like nothing I could've imagined. For starters, I wasn't with the guy I expected to be here. I *was* relieved I hadn't wasted any more time on Kent.

But Dylan was the last man I expected to be having crazy-hot sex with. I was crushing *hard* on him. Sex with Dylan was really good. All things considered, that was convenient because our room wasn't the warmest at night. We were, though.

But it wasn't the sex that had me pondering Jack's observation. What startled me the most was how I felt with Dylan—so encompassed, so protected. I wanted to fall into this and stay there forever with him. Yet I knew his story. He had plenty of good reasons not to want anything remotely resembling commitment. He was also my brother's best friend. By chance, we were both moving to the same town in Alaska. What were the freaking odds of that?

The world was small, and the universe could send people careening into each other's lives like an expert pool shot. My tricky heart had overridden my self-doubt and gone and fallen for Dylan. I wasn't ready to use the word *love*, but wow. I'd never felt like this before.

I kept trying to convince myself it was the situation—the snowstorm, being stuck at this inn with our newfound friends, the cards and games, and the acoustic music in front of the fireplace.

If Jack hadn't gone and said that, I could've persuaded myself to forget it.

Later that night, the band played an early acoustic set. At the end, Lucy made an announcement. "We've gotten an update from the emergency team. The road should be clear first thing tomorrow morning." A little cheer went up in the group. "We'll still be serving breakfast."

When we went to our room, a sense of recklessness stirred inside me. My emotions felt as if they pushed against the surface of my skin—too raw, too fierce, and too intense for me to ignore.

Dylan turned to look at me, and we studied each other. Why did he have to be so handsome?

Despite not shaving for days now, I could still see the cut line of his jaw. He was so strong, so sheltering. I felt tears stinging the backs of my eyes. The ramifications of what had happened inside my heart overwhelmed me.

I wanted to chalk it up to the forbidden quality of this weekend—hot nights with my brother's best friend. I wanted more, enough to soothe the sting of the impending foolish heartbreak.

Emotion tangled up inside of my desire, intensifying it. Everything felt heightened with heat and fire and emotion amplifying each other.

"Well?" Dylan asked.

"Well, what?" I prompted.

"The road will be clear tomorrow."

I blinked, grateful for the dim light. I hoped he couldn't see the tears welling in my eyes. I didn't want this weekend to end. I could've stayed here playing cards with strangers that had become friends and nights tangled up in the chilly room with Dylan under the covers forever.

I swallowed through the emotion thickening in my throat. I felt driven, pushed to find some sort of release valve for all of this. I didn't hesitate to step forward and lean up to kiss him. One of his arms slid around my waist as the other palmed my cheek. He deepened our kiss instantly, holding me in his secure embrace.

That sense of rushing, of recklessness, kept driving me. I yanked at his clothing, and he seemed startled by my fierceness. When I unbuttoned his jeans and knelt to take his thick cock into my mouth, I heard the hiss of his breath through his teeth, followed by, "Piper, we have all night."

That was the crux of the problem. We had *all* night, but *only* tonight.

I paused, lifting my gaze to his. "I know," I whispered before swirling my tongue around his thick crown and sucking him in. He laced his fingers in my hair, tugging lightly while I savored the sting of it. I needed to lose myself in *this*, in the fire of our connection, so I didn't have to think about how the cracks spread across the surface of my heart.

I knew his body now, knew when he was close to his release. His fingers tightened in my hair, and I heard a little growl in his throat. His cock pulsed when I dragged my tongue along the underside before sucking him in once again.

"Piper!" he bit out.

I leaned back, looking up as I released him with a pop. "What?"

"I need to be inside you."

I could've convinced myself it was just sex, just raw lust. But something else was in the look in his eyes. My heart crashed against my ribs.

Several fiery seconds burned by as he tugged me up. We undressed swiftly. Even though it was rushed, I felt cherished with every movement. He tossed my shirt to the side with one hand as his other smoothed down over my hip in a soothing caress. His fingers dug into my skin when he moved me, stretching me out on the bed in front of him. The look in his eyes was almost gentle. I felt as if I was caught in a fire that would never stop burning, the fire itself feeding my need and emotion. I felt stripped bare and cleaved wide open.

He dropped hot kisses over my belly, his fingers teasing along the sensitive skin on the inside of my thigh before he pressed my knee out to the side. He dusted a kiss on the sensitive skin above the inside of my knee. His touch was gentle, like a drop of warm honey. Everything with him was a combination of gentle and intensely sensual.

He teased me to a deep, trembling climax with his mouth and fingers. I was still shuddering from it when he rose up and smoothed a condom on. I welcomed the weight of him coming over me, his hard muscled body, the thick press of his crown at my entrance, the subtle brush of hair on his chest against my breasts, his eyes burning into mine.

I could barely breathe and cried out as one orgasm rolled into the next when he filled me. His slow slide elicited a raw whimper, and I barely recognized myself. I simply handed myself over to him—my heart, all of me, as the sensations washed through me. The waves of pleasure broke with each plunge as he filled me with slow thrusts.

He caught my cry with a kiss when my climax rose to another crashing, piercing crescendo. I felt him go taut as a bow before he jerked once more and shuddered roughly, my name coming in a raspy cry.

We were a tangle of limbs against the pillows. At some point, Dylan left the bed. He returned, dragging the extra blanket over us and pulling me into his arms.

"We have all night," he whispered again.

I pressed a kiss into the divot at the base of his throat, those tears stinging my eyes again.

The following morning, the road was clear, and the inn was a bustle of activity between staff coming in to clean up and guests packing and hustling around to help. We said goodbye to our new friends and exchanged numbers.

Just as he was about to climb into the car, Jack glanced over from where they parked beside us. "Don't forget what I said."

"Huh?" I returned brilliantly.

"I think y'all are meant to be."

I gave him a quick hug. "I won't," I said, keeping my tone light and teasing.

A few minutes later, Dylan closed the trunk, glancing over. "I can drive if you want," he offered.

I shrugged, genuinely not caring one way or the other. "That's fine."

As we began driving away, the sunshine

was blindingly bright, and the sky sharp blue. I looked around as Dylan drove, my eyes taking in the destruction of a swath of trees with rocks tumbled around on both sides of the narrow road where the slide must've occurred.

"What did Jack say?" Dylan asked.

I surprised myself by answering honestly, "He told me not to forget what he said."

"About us?"

My heart gave a funny little pitter-patter in my chest. I glanced over, wishing I could read his mind. I just needed a quick peek inside. I expected him to look amused.

Instead, his gaze was somber. "What do you think about what he said?" he prompted.

My chest tightened, and emotion rose swiftly inside. I glanced out the window. "I don't know, what do you think? You're the one who said you don't believe in love."

When I risked another glance in his direction, he was looking at the road ahead. His jaw clenched tight as his fingers gripped the steering wheel.

"I did. I didn't expect you, Piper Ellis."

"Well, I mean, of course not. You didn't know you would see me after I got ditched at the airport. You didn't even know this weekend was going to happen."

He rounded a curve in the road. Just ahead was a viewing platform off to the side, overlooking a valley.

Dylan pulled the rental car over and parked, facing the view. We looked out over the valley for a moment or so. I took a slow breath, letting it out quietly. I knew these mountains well. The stunning Blue Ridge Mountains were home, where I'd grown up. Even though it was late morning and a bright sunny day, the telltale blue haze was still visible as I looked out over the mountain range.

I'd been out West and knew the mountains there felt different. They were bigger, more of a distant presence. These mountains felt like they cradled you. They were older and had settled into the earth more deeply, surrounding you with little dips and valleys. I looked around, seeing many trees knocked over, some bent permanently from the weight of the ice that had fallen during the recent storm.

Dylan cleared his throat, and I glanced over toward him. My heart started kicking faster, and anxiety spun in my chest.

"What is it?" I asked, my question falling through the soft hum of the heaters blowing into the car.

He turned to face me, and I was startled to see a flicker of uncertainty in his gaze.

"I didn't expect you," he repeated.

I swallowed. "Um, I didn't expect you either."

I wasn't sure where this conversation was going. My pulse kept racing, and the fresh sense of connection and intimacy flickered to life in the air between us.

We sat in a rental car, looking out over a pretty valley. Yet this moment felt suddenly momentous. I felt like I was standing on a precipice, about to leap. Metaphorically speaking and literally, I suppose I was. In another few days, I would get on a plane to Alaska, stepping into a new phase of my life.

"What is it?" I was frightened of the answer and braced myself.

His shoulders rose with a quick breath. "I think I love you."

I had prepared for him to tell me all the obvious things. We were about to visit my brother on the last day before my flight. Meanwhile, Dylan was scheduled to fly out another week after I left for Alaska.

Our lives were intersecting again.

"What?" I sputtered. A soft laugh slipped out.

Dylan reached for my hand where it

rested on the console. He curled his around it, his thumb moving in a soothing stroke across the back. "I said I think I love you."

Joy clamored inside my heart, clanging like a bell with the thrill of it. I was so unprepared for this moment that all I could do was stare at him. "You do?" I finally squeaked.

He looked away for a moment, swallowing before he turned back to face me fully. "I do. You seem surprised, but so am I. I didn't expect this. I didn't expect you. I wouldn't even think it possible, except we've known each other for years."

He studied me quietly, and even though my doubts tried to interrupt, tried to kick the joy flaring my heart into submission, the truth rose through the cacophony. "I think I love you too."

Pesky tears stung my eyes, and I had to swallow through the emotion clogging my throat.

"What should we do about this?" he asked carefully.

I took a quick breath. "Well, we're both going to Alaska."

"Yeah, we are."

"So maybe we..."

"I want to try," he said firmly.

Joy kept banging the drum in my heart as

I smiled through the tears welling in my eyes. "I do too. What are we going to tell Wade?"

Dylan shrugged lightly. "That's up to you. Obviously, I feel like I need to tell him something, but I assume you'll have an opinion about that."

I wasn't ready to tell my brother. This all felt far too fresh. Wade would have more of an opinion than I cared to hear. I didn't want his opinions to interfere with our fragile connection.

"Can we wait? I know we need to tell him at some point. But let's see how things go. Because you know he'll have thoughts."

"Thoughts? He's probably gonna punch me," he offered with a wry smile.

"Let's just go to the lodge. I'll fly out, and then I'll see you in a week. We can tell him after we're both in Alaska."

"Deal," Dylan said before leaning forward and palming my cheek to kiss me fiercely.

Chapter Seventeen

DYLAN

"Hey, hey!" Wade pulled me into a back-slapping hug.

"Hey, man," I returned with a grin as we broke apart.

Piper and I had agreed we'd be honest about running into each other at the airport and spending the weekend together. She said we would just leave out the fact that we'd had "crazy-hot sex." Her words.

I asked her if Wade knew she was meeting her ex for that weekend.

She'd shrugged. "I'll just tell him we broke up at the airport. It's what happened."

I watched as Piper hugged Dani and Wade. We got swept into having lunch at a big picnic table in the back of the staff area at Stolen Hearts Lodge with friends.

Dani, Wade's wife, smiled over at me. "I made your favorite."

"My favorite?"

"That mac and cheese you love so much."

"That is *the* best." I nodded enthusiastically.

"It happens to be Piper's favorite too, so that worked out," Dani added.

"What would you have done if we didn't have the same favorite?" Piper asked.

Dani smiled at us. "I would've made both of your favorites."

Jackson Stone came over, cuffing me lightly on the shoulder as he walked by before he sat down. "Dani likes to take care of everyone. Although we don't usually get that kind of special treatment," he said dryly. Jackson owned Stolen Hearts Lodge, the outdoor resort where Wade worked.

Dani rested her hands on her hips, her ponytail bouncing as she eyed him. "The mac and cheese is pretty much everybody's favorite or, at least, in everybody's top three."

"Definitely my favorite," Shay said as she sat beside Jackson.

Jackson leaned over, giving her a lingering kiss. "Hey, sweetheart," he murmured.

Jackson and Shay had been married for several years now, baby and all.

The lunch carried on around us. Lucas Cole gave me an update about Alaska. Rowan was his cousin and lived there. He'd told me about the opening on the hotshot crew.

All the while, I was acutely aware of the urge to let my gaze linger on Piper. I was relieved we were only here together for one night. I'd be here for the week but didn't know if I could hide my feelings about Piper from Wade for that long.

Shay had put us in guest cabins that happened to be beside each other. I was relieved it was dark when we walked out to them. Only moments after leaving my bag in my cabin, I slipped over to Piper's, and we made love in the darkness.

The next morning, Wade took her to the airport while I stayed back to help Jackson, Dawson, and Walker with a construction project.

I had to say my goodbye to Piper in the morning before the sun even rose. I texted her half an hour before her flight.

Me: *I miss you. I'll see you when you pick me up in Anchorage.*

I had already sent her my flight schedule. As hard as my heart beat out the rhythm of my feelings for her, once she was gone, my doubts began to get louder. What if I couldn't do this? What if all the reasons I told myself commitment was a bad idea turned out to be accurate?

Just because I thought I loved Piper too much to let her slip away didn't mean it wouldn't blow up in my face.

I lay in bed in the darkness the night after she left, missing her and trying not to chase my worries in circles.

Chapter Eighteen

PIPER

Morning, earlier the same day

"Small world," my brother offered from my side as he drove toward the airport.

I glanced over. "Well, yeah, but why do you say that?"

"You and Dylan both moving to Willow Brook just goes to show how small the world can be. That's all."

I quickly looked out the window. "I know. But maybe it's not so small. Rowan is there. We went to high school with Rowan. That's how he knows Dylan." I shrugged, still looking out the window because I didn't want anything on my face to give me away. "Dylan likes to travel. You always say that Alaska is a destination for anyone who likes to hike in the mountains. It's on lots of bucket lists."

"I suppose it's less surprising for me that he's going out there than you," Wade commented.

I finally looked his way again. "Why? I interned with Alice through our vet school. She's from Alaska."

"It's a small world. That's my point. I'm glad Dylan's going to be there. He can keep an eye on you."

Irritation flashed inside. I was doubting my choice to drop off the rental car a few days ago because that meant I'd needed this ride and now, absolutely not to my surprise, my brother was being nosy and over-protective. Ugh. "I don't need anyone to keep an eye on me," I said pointedly, rolling my eyes as I looked away from my overprotective older brother again.

Wade chuckled. "I know you don't, but I worry. It's because I love you. You used to worry about me when I was traveling and hiking and doing my thing."

"I still worry about you." My heart felt warm when I looked over at him.

My brother cast me a quick grin. "It's because you're my sister. You worry about me, and I worry about you, and so on and so on. Shall we bet on how long Dylan will be out there anyway?" he asked lightly.

Anxiety tightened in my chest. "What do you mean?"

"You know him. He never stays anywhere too long, maybe a year or two at best. He is not a man to settle down. Not in where he lives or in romance. He'll never commit. Not to a place or a person," Wade said dryly.

I knew this. I *knew* it. Now, I understood why even more after Dylan told me about his parents. But I didn't want to think about that.

I kept my tone light as I replied, "You never know."

"Oh, I know this," my brother said with confidence. "The longest he's been in one place since college has been maybe a year. He has *never* had a serious relationship."

"Well, you didn't either until you and Dani reconnected," I pointed out.

This conversational path was ridiculous, and I needed an exit ramp.

"Hey, I was serious with Dani in high school," he countered.

I tried to breathe through the tightness in my chest and throat. My brain suddenly had to point out that when Dylan said he loved me, he'd actually said, "I *think* I love you."

Think being the operative word. Of course, I'd said the same thing because I wasn't sure either.

I forced my attention back to Wade. "The best thing is you and Dani found each other again. You never got over her."

"I never did."

My brother's solemn tone caused my heart to twist. He loved Dani thoroughly, the way anyone would want to be loved. He wasn't perfect, she wasn't perfect, but they loved each other, flaws and all.

A few minutes later, Wade pulled into the airport's drop-off area. He gave me a giant bear hug, lifting me in the air before setting me down. "Text me when you get there." He stepped back.

"Of course. Love you, big brother."

A moment later, I walked into the airport as he drove away. I felt lonely. I wished Dylan was coming out to Alaska with me. I had a whole week for my doubts to make a ton of noise in my brain.

Chapter Nineteen

PIPER

Two days later

"What do you think?" Alice asked as she held her arms out and spun in a small circle.

We were in the reception area at the veterinary clinic where I was starting my job as the second veterinarian.

"It's great," I said. And it was. It was a cute little office in downtown Willow Brook, Alaska, with two exam rooms and a surgery room.

Alice's auburn ponytail swung as she turned and smiled back over at me. Just then, Farrah came out of the back area. She was our vet tech and, according to Alice, "kicked ass" at her job.

"We have you all booked up already," Farrah said. "I hope you're ready to hit the ground running."

"Absolutely."

They had scheduled for me to come by and go over questions before my first afternoon here. I hadn't wanted to waste time getting started. The move here wasn't cheap between the travel and the fact that I hadn't worked for a few weeks.

Tiffany, the receptionist, leaned her elbows on the counter surrounding the reception desk. "Don't worry, everything will go smoothly."

Alice grinned at her before adding, "Tiffany is the center of our universe here and runs this whole place. As long as you do exactly what she tells you, you'll be fine."

"I'm great at following instructions," I offered.

I was glad Alice and I had stayed in touch ever since she moved back to Willow Brook. It made it easy to slip back into our friendship. I already felt comfortable with Tiffany and Farrah. It was a breath of fresh air to realize I would be working in a vet clinic staffed entirely by women.

Someone came in with their cat for a scheduled appointment with Alice. Just after that, a family showed up with a limping dog. Tiffany glanced my way, arching a brow in question. "On it."

It felt good to instantly swing into action. Farrah was quick and efficient as a vet tech. It was nothing more than an achy joint for an elderly dog. Beyond the best part of giving the dog lots of love, I made a few suggestions for medication to ease the pain for now and some supplements to help with arthritis.

After the family left, Farrah grinned at me. "You're a perfect fit."

I shadowed Alice for the rest of the afternoon, mostly to get comfortable with the flow of the computer system and get up to speed on where they kept supplies and things along those lines.

We were tidying up at the end of the day when Tiffany smiled at me before glancing between Alice and Farrah. "I think we should go to Wildlands. We can get some burgers, and Piper can see the town."

"What do you think?" Farrah asked.

"I think I'll do whatever y'all want. I'm new to town, I need food, and my apartment is pretty empty," I offered.

Alice had connected me with Farrah to

take over an apartment in her building. Farrah was directly across the hallway with her boyfriend.

"You can ask me if you need anything." Farrah waggled her brows.

"From you and Cooper?" I prompted.

In my afternoon here, I was already filled in on everyone's love life. They were all paired up—coincidentally or not—with fire-fighters.

I had yet to share any info about Dylan. It felt too fresh. Even though we had shared our feelings with each other, that one night in Stolen Hearts Valley hadn't been enough for me to feel confident in us. Doubts were the way I rolled when it came to relationships.

I had told them that my brother's friend, also a firefighter, was moving out here next week. That seemed safe enough.

Tiffany chimed in, "By the way, I asked Wes about Dylan. Wes said he's joining their crew. One of the other guys moved away."

"How many people are on those crews anyway?" I asked, purely out of curiosity.

"Twenty-five," Alice replied. "But Willow Brook houses three crews, so there are fire-fighters everywhere. I think Wildlands is the perfect plan tonight. The guys are meeting there anyway."

Farrah caught my eye. "I'll give you a ride. We can swing by the grocery store afterward so you can get a few things for your apartment. I'll give you rides wherever you need to go until you get a car."

"Is that the plan? To get a car?" Tiffany asked as she slid her arms into a fluffy down jacket.

"That's the plan. But you don't have to give me rides everywhere." I glanced at Farrah. "I can walk. That's one of the convenient things about the apartment. It's right downtown."

"I know," Farrah said as we began walking out together. "But it's winter, and it's cold."

Chapter Twenty

PIPER

Wildlands Restaurant & Bar was decorated with holiday lights, reflecting in a blurry shimmer on the icy lake behind the lodge.

We walked in together, and I glanced around. Aside from this being a hotel, there was a large restaurant and bar. The restaurant area had hardwood flooring and exposed wooden beams. The ceiling was high, creating a sense of space.

Alice walked beside me, and I followed them to a table where some people were already seated. After a round of introductions, I sat down, and Jonah, who I'd already met since he was married to Alice, smiled at me.

"I hear a friend of yours is joining our crew?" he prompted.

"I believe so. I guess—" I paused just as someone tapped my shoulder. I glanced up to see Rowan Cole. "Rowan!" I stood and gave him a quick hug.

"Hey there, Piper. I can now officially text your brother and tell him I've seen you, and you're here safe and sound," Rowan teased.

I chuckled. "Did Wade seriously ask you to text him?"

He gave me an apologetic smile. "He sure did."

I rolled my eyes. "Of course he did."

I sat down again, my brain swimming by the many introductions of people. At one point, I leaned over to Alice seated beside me. "You all have a lot of friends, and there are *a lot* of firefighters."

She grinned. "There are. You know how it is with small towns. I visited you in Stolen Hearts Valley once during the summer. You eventually get to know lots of people."

I liked the sense of camaraderie and friendship. It was different but also similar to Stolen Hearts Valley. That night, I lay in my bed in my new apartment. I missed Dylan but also felt a curl of anticipation. He would be here in a week, and maybe, just maybe, our flourishing relationship could actually become real.

He had texted me to check in multiple times today. I'd kept him updated and sent him a few photographs of the town and my apartment.

I just hoped the feelings would hold. The further away we got from that weekend at the inn, the more it felt like a mirage.

Chapter Twenty-One

PIPER

"So how's it going?" Wade asked.

I sat at the small round table in my apartment while talking with him on the phone. I looked out over Main Street at the snow-covered mountains in the distance and the cute little town with its colorful storefronts.

"Good so far. Did you seriously ask Rowan to give you an update?"

"Of course," Wade said easily. "Him and Delilah."

"Oh my God," I grumbled. I wanted to ask how Dylan was. Badly. But I didn't want to cue Wade into curiosity about why I was asking. My brother could be too perceptive sometimes.

Whether or not he knew what I was

thinking, he spoke, offering, "Dylan will be out there next week. He's sowing the last of his oats here before he goes. He's staying true to form."

"Huh?"

"His old situationship, Tonya, was here at the lodge last night. You know Dylan. It's never more than a night."

My gut twisted bitterly. The disappointment I expected pierced my heart.

"Oh," I said.

My throat ached and my eyes stung. I didn't want Wade to suspect anything, so I exclaimed, "Oh! I just realized the time. I've gotta go." I was lying, but I didn't care.

I got off the phone just as a text came in from Dylan.

Dylan: *How's day three?*

I stared at my phone screen. Maybe it was impulsive, but I decided I didn't want to drag this out. It was better if I reset everything right now.

Me: *I've been thinking. I think it's best if we just forget everything that happened. It was just a weekend.*

As soon as I sent the text, I turned my phone off. I had to go to work anyway. There was no sense in even trying to have a dialogue about this.

It was a full two hours later at the clinic when I finally turned my phone back on.

Dylan: *What the hell is going on? What are you talking about?*

He'd sent the next text only a minute after that.

Dylan: *At least give me the decency of an explanation.*

I took a shaky breath.

Me: *Tonya.*

I knew who Tonya was. I remembered one of the times Dylan had visited Wade before. He'd spent a night with her. Even though I thought he was totally cute and sort of crushed on him then, it hadn't hurt. Because I was a sensible girl.

My phone rang. I stared at Dylan's name flashing on the screen with every ring. I took a fortifying breath and slid my thumb across the screen to answer.

"Hi."

"Nothing happened with Tonya," Dylan said.

"Wade mentioned it. It's fine, Dylan. It's probably for the best. Maybe we just got caught up in the emotion of the weekend between the holidays and the storm. You told me you had your reasons for never wanting to get serious anyway."

My heart ached with every word.

"Piper—"

I didn't even let him go on and cut in. "I have to go."

A single tear rolled down my cheek. Just then, Tiffany came walking into the break room. As soon as she saw me, her perceptive gaze narrowed.

"What happened?" She stood in front of me in an instant, flinging her arms around me in a big hug. In the few days I'd been here, I had already discovered Tiffany was loving and affectionate and wanted to take care of everyone.

When she stepped back, she squeezed my shoulders. "Tell me what happened," she insisted.

I hedged. "Don't you have to be out front? I'm just being silly."

"No, it's lunch. Remember, we actually take lunch here. It's kind of a thing."

Before I knew it, Farrah and Alice had appeared, and we were all sitting around the table. I told them everything, ending with, "And it's just so stupid. I shouldn't have let anything happen."

Alice sat beside me and curled her arm around my shoulders, leaning close with a squeeze. When she leaned back, she said, "It happened. Are you sure about what Wade said?"

I nodded. "I mean, it's what I would expect." I took a shaky breath. "I just wish Dylan wasn't moving here."

"Maybe you should call your brother and clarify," Farrah suggested.

My mouth fell open as I sputtered, "Are you crazy? I don't want to think about what my brother will say if I tell him I had a fling with his best friend. No, thank you. I don't need a lecture from Wade. I love my brother, but he can be an asshole about things like that. I already had to explain the whole thing with getting ditched at the airport."

Alice cocked her head to the side. "We're here for you. I'll tell you right now that Dylan won't be off to a good start in this town."

Tiffany snorted. "And what exactly are you going to do, Alice?"

"I don't know. Tell him he's an asshole," Alice retorted.

Tiffany chuckled. I smiled even though my heart ached. I felt incredibly foolish, but I smiled among my friends. "Good to know you've got my back."

Chapter Twenty-Two

DYLAN

"What gives?" Wade asked as he eyed me from across the table.

I was having dinner with him and Dani. Dani hadn't gotten home yet, but I had come out to help him move a new couch into their living room and carry the old one onto the sunporch Wade had built over the summer.

"What do you mean?" I hedged.

"You looked, uh, worried, I guess, all afternoon."

I contemplated my options here. Piper would probably skin me alive if I told Wade about us, but I needed to figure out what the hell was going on. Tonya had stopped by Stolen Hearts Lodge restaurant the other night unexpectedly, but absolutely *nothing* other than a brief conversation had happened.

I'd walked her out to her car, and that was it. My best guess was Wade might've assumed just because she stopped and chatted with me for a few minutes that something happened. Now, I didn't know what the fuck to do.

Every time I thought about dropping it and letting Piper go, a sense of panic churned. I still couldn't quite believe it, but I had fallen in love with Piper. No matter how loud my doubts were, I didn't care. I was willing to pay the price of loss if that's what happened in the long run, but I wasn't ready to let her go without a fight.

"Dylan?" Wade prompted, tapping his fingertips on the table.

I lifted my gaze to his and cleared my throat. "So before I say this, you can punch me."

My friend's brow furrowed in confusion. "Why the hell would I want to punch you?"

I decided to lead with the important part. "I love Piper."

His brows flew up in confusion. "Piper? My sister?"

I cleared my throat again. "Yes, Piper,

your sister. The only Piper I know. I love her."

Wade was still not getting the memo. He cocked his head to the side, narrowing his eyes. "You love Piper? Like romantic love?"

My heart thudded against my ribs an answer. "Yes."

I could see the tension in Wade's shoulders. "What the fuck? So what the hell happened with Tonya the other night?"

"Nothing. Absolutely nothing. We talked about the weather, and I asked how she was doing. I walked her out to her car, and that was it." Wade rolled his eyes. "The only reason I'm saying anything to you—and Piper asked me not to, by the way—is because apparently, you told her something happened with Tonya and me. I don't know what the fuck you told her, but now she won't even talk to me."

"How do I know nothing happened with you and Tonya?"

"I have no reason to lie to you about this," I said flatly.

"Well, actually you do. You're trying to get me to cover for you with Piper."

"I'm not trying to get you to cover for anything. Nothing happened!" I exclaimed. "Hold on a sec. Ask Evie and Dawson. They saw me come back in by myself, and I sat down with them. I'm calling Dawson right now." I slid my phone out of my pocket, pulling his number up, and calling him.

"Hey, what's up?" Dawson asked by way of greeting

"You're on speaker. Could you please tell Wade that after I walked Tonya to her car, I came right back into the restaurant the other night?"

"Sure. I know you did because you sat with us. I don't know what this is about, but I can vouch for that," Dawson said.

"Thank you. Catch you later."

I tapped the screen to end the call and crossed my arms as I studied my best friend. Wade stretched his jaw in an effort to ease the tension. His expression was thunderous.

"I can't believe you fucked my little sister. Oh my God, I can't even believe I said that sentence." He ran his hands through his hair, just as the door to the kitchen opened from the side entrance, and Dani came walking in.

Her gaze flicked back and forth between us. "What's going on?"

Wade looked over at her. "He was with Piper that weekend." He flung his hand in the air, gesturing toward me. "Says he loves her."

Dani didn't even flinch. She set her purse on the table by the door and hung her jacket on a hook before she walked over to Wade. Hands on her hips, she eyed him. "Calm down." Her gaze lifted to me. "I knew something was up with you and Piper."

"You did?!" Wade exclaimed.

Dani looked his way, her expression understanding. "I didn't know what exactly. That's why I didn't say anything. It could've just been a vibe, a crush."

Wade sighed heavily. "Great. Well, Dylan wants me to straighten things out with Piper because I mentioned he had a thing with Tonya the other night."

"Yeah, why would you say that? Nothing even happened. He came back into the restaurant. Dylan's your friend. Cut him some slack."

Dani totally had my back. I stood. "Give me a hug, bring it in." I held my arms open.

Dani laughed as she gave me a quick hug. As she stepped back, her gaze sobered. "I've got your back on Tonya, but you better not hurt Piper." Her eyes narrowed.

"I love her."

"I don't even know how you can know that," Dani said pointedly.

Since I was all in on being honest, I kept

at it. "Because I've known her for years. Things were really intense."

"Oh my fucking God! I did *not* need to know how intense it was," Wade practically spat out.

Dani glanced over at me, giving me a stern look. It was a weak effort because she was about to burst out laughing. She lost the battle, though, when a laugh finally sputtered out.

Wade glared at her. "Seriously? I think you would be on my side with this." He gestured to me. "This guy has never been in a serious relationship. Never." He jabbed his forefinger into the table in emphasis.

Dani's gaze was somber as she looked from me to Wade. "I know. But he's also never been an asshole. You just heard me threaten him if he hurts Piper. I'm with you there. But Dylan's your best friend. I don't think he'd be stupid enough to say he loved Piper to your face if he didn't actually *love* Piper."

Although Wade's comments stung a little, I understood his point. "You're not wrong," I replied. "But neither is Dani. I'm not an asshole." I paused, closing my eyes and taking a breath to slow the anxiety churning in my chest. When I opened them again, I added, "I've never felt like this about anyone. I'm as surprised as you. I don't even know if Piper believes me." I threw my hands up in the air. "Her reaction to this shows me maybe she doesn't. I'm gonna have to prove it to her. I could use an assist from you, though. Do you believe now that nothing happened with me and Tonya?"

Wade gritted his teeth before opening his mouth wide and stretching his jaw. "Yes," he grumbled. "Let's call her."

"Now?"

Dani waggled her brows.

"Buckle up, buttercup," Wade said dryly. "If you're going to be with my sister, you're gonna have to deal with the fact I know about it."

I swallowed. "Piper's going to fucking kill me that I told you anything about us."

"Why?" Wade asked sharply.

"Because she specifically asked me not to tell you. She wasn't ready."

"Hmm." Wade shrugged slowly. "Better her pissed at you than me."

Before I could protest further, he snagged his phone off the edge of the table and tapped it to call, putting it on speaker.

My heart banged along unsteadily on my

chest. I could barely breathe waiting for Piper to answer.

After a moment, her voice came through the line. "Hey, Wade."

My heart twisted in my chest.

"You're on speaker," he replied.

"Um, okay," Piper said slowly. "Is Dani there with you?"

"Oh, I'm here," Dani offered. "For the record, I don't agree with this plan."

"What plan?" Piper asked, sounding suspicious.

"I'm here with Dani and Dylan. Dylan asked me to call you and clarify that he was not with Tonya the other night. I have verified this from an independent source." Wade glared at me briefly. "She came over to chat with him at the lodge restaurant, and I saw them go out to the parking lot, at which point I left. Dawson has verified that Dylan came back inside within a few minutes."

"Dylan is there now?" Piper's tone was sharp enough to cut me.

I cleared my throat. "Yeah, I'm here."

There was a beat of loaded silence. "Okay. Is that all?" Piper asked.

"I just want to add that Dani and I have threatened Dylan's life if he hurts you. Love you, sis." His thumb hovered over the screen.

"Wade!" Piper said.

"You'll have to sort this out with Dylan."

"It was Wade's idea to do this stupid group call! Love you!" Dani said quickly.

When Wade threw her a glare, she shrugged. "It *was* your idea. I got your back, but on this, you should be honest. Don't blame Dylan for something that was your idea."

"Love you, sis," Wade said. "Would you like to talk to Dylan?"

"No, thank you," Piper said, her tone icy and polite.

"Piper—" I began.

The line went dead.

I looked at Wade. "Fuck," I muttered.

My best friend shrugged, rolling his eyes. "Good luck with Piper."

Chapter Twenty-Three

DYLAN

I left, contemplating my next steps to repair the rift with Piper. Maybe I could understand that this was fast for us, but what I said to Wade was accurate. I'd known Piper for years. Since Wade was my best friend, we'd visited each other many times. Every time Piper was around, I'd done my damnedest not to notice how freaking cute she was.

I understood her doubts. I just had to prove her wrong. I wanted to call her, but I knew that wouldn't be enough. I sent her one text.

Me: *I love you. I know you're pissed that I talked to Wade about us, but I was desperate. I'll see you soon. I love you.*

I figured some things were worth repeating.

Chapter Twenty-Four

PIPER

"Oh, so now you're pissed at him because he talked to your brother," Alice said, nodding slowly.

"Well, that totally makes sense," Farrah chimed in, her tone dry as chalk.

I looked at my friends. "What?"

I'd only been working at the clinic for a few days and already felt close to Farrah and Tiffany. It was easy and comfortable. Alice was the bridge from me to them, and they were awesome, funny, and smart. While my heart was breaking into pieces over Dylan, they encircled me with support and love. Just the kind of friends a girl needed.

"Why did you say it like that?" I added, feeling a little defensive.

Farrah pursed her lips, letting out a little puff of air and rolling her eyes. "Because. Okay, let's rewind to when you thought he had a one-night stand with someone. Whatever. Fair enough. But that didn't happen. He was panicking, and your brother was the one who unintentionally gave you the inaccurate information. How was Dylan going to straighten it out without involving your brother?"

"Not to mention the obvious fact that Wade will find out at some point anyway," Alice interjected.

I sighed. "I don't know. I just wanted more time before I talked to Wade. He's nosy and overprotective, and he always has an opinion, and that's—" I paused, sighing. "I don't know."

"So he plays the stereotype as the older brother," Farrah replied. "My guess is you're a nosy sister who's also overprotective."

"I know we've only known each other a few days, but it sure seems like Dylan means a lot to you. Maybe give him a chance," Tiffany said gently.

Tiffany's words played on a loop in my thoughts that night when I was alone in my apartment. I'd only gotten one text from Dylan since the call with Wade. Because I was feeling snippy about him talking to Wade, I hadn't even replied yet.

I jumped when there was a sharp knock on my door. I turned around and stared at the door from where I stood by the kitchen counter. There was another knock, and I practically felt the echo of it in my heart. I strolled over to the door. Farrah and Cooper were out to dinner tonight, so I didn't think it was Farrah. I already loved living across the hall from someone friendly and having a neighbor who checked on me.

Maybe it was Janet, my landlady. I opened the door, and my heart about beat its way out of my chest when I saw Dylan standing there. I literally jumped, my palm flying to my chest.

"Oh! What are you doing here?" I yelped.

Dylan stood there, his gaze locked with mine. "I missed you, so I changed my flight."

"But you're early," I said pointlessly.

"I am. Can I come in?"

Before I could think it through, my body decided for me. I stepped back and pulled the door open for him to walk through. After he came in, he stood just inside the door.

"How did you know where my apartment was?" I asked slowly, lacing my hands together and rubbing my thumb on the inside of my other palm, a nervous habit.

"I had to do a little reconnaissance. I got ahold of Rowan, who told me where you were staying. I also found out that apparently, half my new crew thinks I'm an asshole because I screwed around on you." He sighed, running a hand through his hair. "I didn't. I love you. And maybe showing up early isn't much of a gesture, but I'll make one every day until you believe me."

Chapter Twenty-Five

PIPER

My heart felt like hands clapping in my chest as I stared up at Dylan. I couldn't even grasp how this had happened. I had fallen in love with him.

While my emotions felt like a train racing at full speed, I *knew* him. I'd known him for years. All we needed was the intensity of that weekend with a snowstorm and being stranded together to forget about the barriers between us.

I scrambled, trying to find something to cling to, something to keep me sane.

"I can't believe you told Wade," I said.

There was a glint in Dylan's eyes, and his lips teased with a smile. "I had to. He's the one who gave you the wrong idea."

I took a slow breath. "I know. How did he react?"

"He was pissed. He threatened me bodily harm if I hurt you in any way. So did Dani." Dylan shrugged, not even the least bit bothered about that.

I had to bite the inside of my cheeks to keep from laughing. "Ha! I'd be more afraid of Dani than Wade. Oh, for sure, he could hit you harder, just based on physics. But she would twist the knife."

Dylan chuckled. "I don't doubt she would." His gaze sobered as he studied me. "How are you?"

I took a shaky breath. "Better."

He stepped a little closer, his hand sliding along the counter to hook his pinky into mine. "Yeah?"

My chest was tight with my heartbeat pounding so hard I could barely hear over the rush of it. My body felt as if it were racing, hurtling down a hill. I couldn't slow the momentum. I was along for the ride.

"I'm better, but I was really hurt," I finally said, deciding to be direct. "Everything felt really fresh for us, and it all took me off guard."

His eyes held mine, never once looking away. "I know."

My throat ached, and I tried to swallow. Tears pricked the backs of my eyes, and I prayed I wouldn't burst into a messy bout of crying. Emotion rose swiftly, jamming up in my chest. I blinked, and tears splashed onto my cheeks.

Dylan's eyes widened in alarm. He stepped closer. "Hey, hey," he soothed in a gruff tone. "Please don't cry, Piper."

I blinked rapidly, wiping the tears away from beneath my eyes with my fingertips as I took another shaky breath. "I guess I'm feeling my way through this," I managed with a sniffle.

"I think we both are." He paused, his gaze somber. "Are you willing to try? With me?"

I nodded, tucking my head into the curve of his shoulder as he pulled me into his arms. He wrapped me in his strong, protective embrace and simply held me for a few minutes. I needed it. I needed to breathe him in, to feel his presence again. I started to settle inside, and I finally lifted my head.

With one arm wrapped firmly around my waist, he raised his other hand to smooth my hair back from my cheeks. "I've missed you, Piper."

His forehead fell to mine briefly before he angled his head to the side and dusted his lips over mine. It was a brief touch, but I could feel the electricity of our connection, almost hearing the snap and crackle of it in the air as it shimmied to life around us, and need and emotion tangled together.

I made a little sound in my throat, something like a whimper before I whispered his name.

On the heels of another breath, he fit his mouth over mine. This was a slow, lingering, consuming kiss. By the time we broke apart to breathe, my body felt like it was on fire, spinning with sensations.

I was caught in his gaze as he whispered, "I love you, Piper."

Roaring emotion crashed over me. I stared up at him. My reply was caught with the word "love" fusing between our lips.

It had been mere days since we'd been together, yet somehow it felt as if we had journeyed miles upon miles in both time and distance. We were in a hurry to get close. Our connection had been forged in the fire of our physical intimacy, and that was what grounded us again.

It was a rush, a messy, stumbling few moments as we tossed our clothes aside. Surprisingly, we made it to the bedroom. When I sank down over him as we mapped each others' bodies, reconnecting with glancing touches, teasing fingers, and hot, open kisses, I felt as if we were coming home together.

He whispered, "Stay with me, look at me. I want to see you right now."

I was ensnared in his starlight-blue gaze. He held me close when I flew apart, pleasure ricocheting through me. I heard his rough cry as he followed me a moment later.

After that intense reconnection, our night was rather mundane. We showered and ordered takeout together when Dylan declared he was starving. We curled up on the couch and watched television and ate pizza before we fell asleep. It was exactly what I needed.

EPILOGUE

Dylan

Almost a year later

"I'm who?" I prompted.

"Dilly Dylan," Maisie Steele announced with a bright smile as her brown curls bounced around her shoulders.

Maisie was the main dispatcher and receptionist and all-around everything at Willow Brook Fire & Rescue in Alaska.

Rowan happened to be standing beside me. I had just learned Maisie had nicknames for everybody in her contacts. Rowan clapped me on the shoulder. "I'll just start calling you Dilly."

Beck, Maisie's husband and also a hotshot

firefighter on a different crew here, snorted from my other side. "She's not very creative. Everybody's name is like that. There's Wessy Wes, Rowy Rowan, and so on and so forth."

"At least you're not Grammy Graham," Graham Holden said as he came through the doorway from the back hall.

"I should just start calling everybody by their nickname," Maisie said with a grin as she glanced among us.

"Beck is the only one with something different," Cooper offered from Rowan's other side as he rested his elbows on the counter encircling Maisie's command center.

"What's your name in her contacts?" I glanced at Beck.

Maisie bit her bottom lip as she giggled.

"Go ahead and tell him," Beck said dryly.

"Beck action hero Steele," she said solemnly.

There was a round of laughter. "So we should just call you action hero?" I prompted.

Beck let out a belabored sigh. "So, Carrie Dodge, you know the lady whose cats get stuck in a tree every few months?"

"Oh yeah, I went out for that once."

"It's basically a training exercise at this point. Anyway, one time Carrie called me that, and it stuck," he explained sheepishly. "And now it's in Maisie's phone."

Maisie shrugged lightly. "Hotshot firefighters are basically all action heroes, but I can only call Beck that. So the rest of you..." She waggled her brows. "Dilly, Coopy, Grammy, and Rowy, well, that's what you get."

After a few more minutes of low-key teasing conversation, the group broke apart. I walked through the back area, swinging by my locker to grab my keys.

The biggest adjustment for me in Alaska was the short days in winter and the long days in summer. Being in the southern part of the state, I discovered we didn't experience full darkness during the winter. The sun sure came up later than I was accustomed to in winter, and summer days were seriously long with only a few hours of darkness.

I left the station, hopping in my truck to pick Piper up from the vet clinic. The moment I thought of her, my lips curled into a smile. I stayed with her almost every night lately, and I loved it.

The following morning, I held the door to the coffee shop as Piper brushed past me, letting out a happy sigh. She smiled up at me as I closed the door behind us. "It's warm in here," she announced.

"Well, the upside to it being fucking cold outside is all we have to do is walk inside, and it feels warm."

Piper nudged me with her elbow. I leaned down to kiss her, feeling her lips curling in a smile against mine before she drew back.

"No, but it's really warm in here. It's early, and I know Janet's got the ovens baking in the back."

"I sure do," Janet said, hearing Piper's reply as we approached the counter at Firehouse Café.

Janet chuckled as she glanced back and forth between us. In the year since I had moved to Willow Brook, Alaska, I'd discovered this café was the pulse of the town and Janet was everybody's unofficial mother. With her warm, brown eyes and silver-streaked dark hair, usually twisted into a braid, a smile from her was enough to brighten any day.

"What brings you two here so early?" she asked as her eyes bounced to the clock on the wall that read 6:00 a.m.

"Is that a judgment on when we usually get here?" I teased.

Janet shrugged. "No, but..." She slid her gaze to Piper. "Is he a late sleeper?"

Piper arched a brow as she glanced up at me. "Not really. He gets up earlier than me. We're here early because Dylan said we had somewhere to be. I have no idea where we have to be by six-thirty in the morning." Her gaze turned pointed.

"Ah," Janet said. "Well, wherever you have to be, you obviously need coffee first."

We got our coffees. Piper got her favorite cranberry scone, and I got an everything bagel. I had a surprise for her.

We had already talked about making it official and moving in together. Piper's lease was coming up on her apartment. We planned to fly to Stolen Hearts Valley for the upcoming holidays and spend the weekend at the pub where it had all begun. Piper had jokingly said she hoped we got stranded again because it was fun. It *was* fun.

But first, I had a surprise.

I'd been renting a place from Russell, a fellow hotshot firefighter. I'd also been working on a secret project.

I knew what I wanted in life: Piper, and to stay here. She loved her job, I loved mine, and life was pretty freaking good these days.

She bounced her heels on the floorboard

of my truck as I drove. "Where are we going?"

I grinned over at her. "Just wait. We're almost there."

I'd found a sweet piece of property just outside downtown Willow Brook. There was no house there yet, but there would be. Probably next summer if I had my way as far as using the winter to plan and then start building in the spring before fire season kept me away too much.

A few minutes later, I rolled my truck to a stop. There was already a driveway and a foundation here.

I took a moment to look around. The foundation where the house would eventually be was situated perfectly on a low rise. The mountains were visible in the distance, although that was pretty much the case no matter where you were in Willow Brook. There was a small pond to the side, and I envisioned a deck off the back of the house that would give us a pretty view.

Piper glanced at me. "Where are we? I mean, it's pretty, but..."

I gestured at the foundation. "See that?"

"Yeah," she said slowly.

"Come on."

I hopped out of the truck, and she followed. I reached for her hand. We walked to the foundation and stopped. "I bought this piece of property. For us. The foundation is here already because someone was going to build here and had to move unexpectedly. I heard about it from Cade at the station. The people had originally hired Amelia to build it," I said, referring to Cade's wife, who ran a construction business and was friends with Piper.

Piper stared at the foundation, her eyes wide and bright when they shifted to me. "For us?"

I turned to face her fully, reaching for her other hand. I lifted one, brushing a kiss across the back. I had actually planned this part. Maybe it's because I'd been thinking about it so much.

"I told you almost a year ago that I fell in love with you. We've had this whole year together. We're talking about moving in together, so let's just skip to being married and building our life together. I only want you. The foundation is here, so we're stuck with the shape of it, although we could change it if we wanted. Let's build this house together. Let's make it ours."

Piper's mouth dropped open. "What?!"

she sputtered. She blinked quickly, her eyes glistening with a sheen of tears.

I dropped one of her hands and palmed her cheek. "I love you, Piper Ellis, and I want to spend the rest of my life with you. What do you say?"

After an electric silence, she squealed and threw her arms around me, her "yes" muffled when she tucked her head into the curve of my shoulder. I caught her fast in my arms and spun around.

If we were going to build a home together, we would build a life together.

We walked around the property until Piper shivered. I dragged her back into my truck and drove back to her apartment.

Later that night, she looked over at me. "So you'll move in here. We'll just sign this lease for the next year. That makes sense because we have to build the house."

"Everything makes sense with you, Piper. I think that storm last winter was meant to be."

To read other stories set at the rustic Merry Falls Lodge, look for books with the Merry Ever After icon from the following authors:

Elena Aitken, J.H. Croix, Erika Kelly, Erin Nicholas, Kait Nolan

You can find them all here: https://www.subscribepage.com/merryeverafter

Thank you for reading Piper & Dylan's story! Want a glimpse of the future for them? Join my newsletter to receive an exclusive scene.

Sign up here: https://BookHip.com/HFMRBGX

p.s. If you are already subscribed, you'll still be able to access the scene.

Up next in the Fireweed Harbor Series is One More Time.

McKenna ends up with a black eye when she meets Jack. Sort of, but not really, his fault.

Black eye aside, the earth shakes when she meets him. But McKenna only believes in love for other people. Unlucky might as well be her middle name.

Jack doesn't care about luck and he's a

breath-stealing, swoony hotshot firefighter. He can't forget McKenna, although she makes him forget plenty of other things.

Don't miss McKenna & Jack's swoony, hot and intense romance!

Pre-order One More Time - due out February 2024!

For more swoony romance...

This Crazy Love kicks off the Swoon Series - small town southern romance with enough heat to melt you! Jackson & Shay's story is epic - swoon-worthy & intensely emotional. Jackson just happens to be Shay's brother's best friend. He's also *seriously* easy on the eyes. Shay has a past, the kind of past she would most definitely like to forget. Past or not, Jackson is about to rock her world. Don't miss their story! Free on all retailers!

Burn For Me is a second chance romance for the ages. Sexy firefighters? Check. Rugged men? Check. Wrapped up together? Check. Brave the fire in this hot, small-town romance. Amelia & Cade were high school sweethearts & then it all fell apart. When

they cross paths again, it's epic - don't miss
Cade's story!
Free on all retailers!

For more small town romance, take a visit to
Last Frontier Lodge in Diamond Creek. A
sexy, alpha SEAL meets his match with a
brainy heroine in Take Me Home. Marley is
all brains & Gage is all brawn. Sparks fly
when their worlds collide. Don't miss Gage &
Marley's story!
Free on all retailers!

If sports romance lights your spark, check
out The Play. Liam is a British footballer
who falls for Olivia, his doctor. A twist of
forbidden heats up this swoon-worthy &
laugh-out-loud romance. Don't miss Liam &
Olivia's story.
Free on all retailers!

FIND MY BOOKS

Thank you for reading Meant To Be! I hope you enjoyed the story. If so, you can help other readers find my books in a variety of ways.

1) Write a review!
2) Sign up for my newsletter, so you can receive information about upcoming new releases & receive a FREE copy of one of my books: http://jhcroixauthor.com/subscribe/
3) Like and follow my Amazon Author page at https://amazon.com/author/jhcroix
4) Follow me on Bookbub at https://www.bookbub.com/authors/j-h-croix

5) Follow me on Instagram at <u>https://www.
instagram.com/jhcroix/</u>
6) Like my Facebook page at <u>https://www.
facebook.com/jhcroix</u>

———

Fireweed Harbor Series
Make You Mine
Dare To Fall
Be The One
Light My Fire Series
Wild With You
Hold Me Now
Only Ever Us
Fall For Me
Keep Me Close
With Every Breath
All It Takes
Take Me Now
Meant To Be
Dare With Me Series
Crash Into You
Evers & Afters
Come To Me
Back To Us
Take Me There
After We Fall
Swoon Series

This Crazy Love
Wait For Me
Break My Fall
Truly Madly Mine
Still Go Crazy
If We Dare
Steal My Heart
Into The Fire Series
Burn For Me
Slow Burn
Burn So Bad
Hot Mess
Burn So Good
Sweet Fire
Play With Fire
Melt With You
Burn For You
Crash & Burn
That Snowy Night
Brit Boys Sports Romance
The Play
Big Win
Out Of Bounds
Play Me
Naughty Wish
Diamond Creek Alaska Novels
When Love Comes
Follow Love
Love Unbroken

<u>Love Untamed</u>
<u>Tumble Into Love</u>
<u>Christmas Nights</u>
Last Frontier Lodge Novels
<u>Take Me Home</u>
<u>Love at Last</u>
<u>Just This Once</u>
<u>Falling Fast</u>
<u>Stay With Me</u>
<u>When We Fall</u>
<u>Hold Me Close</u>
<u>Crazy For You</u>
<u>Just Us</u>

ACKNOWLEDGMENTS

Thank you to my readers, to my assistant, to my cover designer, to my author friends, to my family and to the universe for giving me a chance to write stories and send them out into the world. Thank you, thank you, thank you.

This story was written during a challenging time, so I'm grateful to even have it out in the wilds.

xoxo
J.H. Croix

ABOUT THE AUTHOR

USA Today Bestselling Author J. H. Croix lives in a small town with her husband and two spoiled dogs. Croix writes contemporary romance with sassy women and alpha men who aren't afraid to show some emotion. Her love for quirky small-towns and the characters that inhabit them shines through in her writing. Take a walk on the wild side of romance with her bestselling novels!

Places you can find me:
jhcroixauthor.com
jhcroix@jhcroix.com

facebook.com/jhcroix
instagram.com/jhcroix
bookbub.com/authors/j-h-croix